SOME DAY
I'LL FIND YOU

SOME DAY
I'LL FIND YOU

Donna Baker

G.K. Hall & Co. • Chivers Press
Thorndike, Maine USA   Bath, England

13 8 1602

This Large Print edition is published by G.K. Hall & Co., USA
and by Chivers Press, England.

Published in 1999 in the U.S. by arrangement with
Chivers Press Ltd.

Published in 1999 in the U.K. by arrangement with
Severn House Publishers, Ltd.

U.S. Hardcover   0-7838-8475-3   (Romance Series Edition)
U.K. Hardcover   0-7540-1254-9   (Windsor Large Print)
U.K. Softcover   0-7540-2185-8   (Paragon Large Print)

The text of this Large Print edition is unabridged.
Other aspects of the book may vary from the original edition.

Set in 16 pt. Plantin by Rick Gundberg.

Printed in the United States on permanent paper.

British Library Cataloguing in Publication Data available

Library of Congress Cataloging in Publication Data

Baker, Donna.
   Some day I'll find you / Donna Baker.
     p. cm.
   ISBN 0-7838-8475-3 (lg. print : hc. : alk. paper)
   1. Large type books. I. Title.
   [PS3552.A414S56 1999]
   813′.54—dc21
                                             98-49001

SOME DAY
I'LL FIND YOU

Chapter One

Crete

Alix Berringer settled back into her seat, her heart beating a little fast. It didn't seem too long since she'd been in another aircraft, on her way to New Zealand. And it was the story her grandfather had told her on that trip that had brought her here now, in search of the answer to a question that had hung in his mind for over fifty years. In search of a lost love . . .

Alix opened her bag and took out the little sheaf of papers her grandfather had given her. His photograph, taken when he was about twenty, tall and smiling in his army uniform. Impossibly young, she thought, to be going to war — yet that was what he and thousands like him had done. Australians and New Zealanders, coming to Crete to protect the island from the Germans — and then, hurriedly evacuated, forced to leave the island to the mercy of the enemy.

She remembered the stories he had told her. Of submarines surfacing under cover of darkness, taking aboard all the men who could be rowed out to them by the Cretans who had sheltered them at risk of their own lives. Of the monastery which had hidden them, the families who

7

had taken the soldiers in, fighting alongside them in their efforts to beat off the invaders.

Of Iphigenia . . .

She looked at the sketch her grandfather had given her. It was a copy, for he had not been able to bear to let the original out of his hands, but it was clear enough. He had drawn it himself, he told Alix, while Iphigenia sat before him, gazing at him with the expression he loved so much. A Cretan beauty, no more than eighteen or nineteen years old, her dark hair falling in loose waves about her shoulders, her eyes smouldering and sooty, her full lips pouting as if waiting for a kiss . . .

Had the Cretan beauty spent the past fifty years still waiting for her lover, wondering why he had left her, why he had never come back? Or did she think him dead and spend her life mourning him, shadowed by the tragedy of a love that could never be?

Ian McConnell had never known. And now, an old man of seventy-five, almost crippled by arthritis, his one wish was to find the girl he had loved so long ago, and to tell her why he had never come back. To finish what had been started and then left, Alix thought, suddenly aware of a parallel with her own life. He too had known the frustration of unfinished business — and, what was more, he recognised that Iphigenia herself must have felt it too. For the mission with which he had entrusted Alix was as much on the Cretan girl's behalf as on his own.

"I'd have done it myself if I'd been fit," he'd told her as they sat in his garden in Auckland, overlooking the blue waters of the bay. "But my travelling days are past. Anyway, there's no way I could've done it while your grandma was alive. But now — well, I keep thinking about her, wondering what happened to her all those years ago. They had a pretty rough time on Crete during the war, after we'd gone, and I reckon a lot of us didn't feel too happy about that. Sorta felt we'd run out on them, y'see." He sighed, looking down at the bright sails of the boats dancing on the waves. "I used to wonder if she'd even survived the war. By the time it was all over a few years had gone by, and when she never got in touch . . ."

"Didn't you ever try to find out?" Alix asked. "Didn't you write?"

Her grandfather shook his head. "We'd agreed she should be the one to make contact. She was engaged, y'see — betrothed, they called it — but it was an arranged marriage and she never really loved him. Didn't even think of it — it was the way things were done, a girl was supposed to make a good marriage with the feller her parents had picked out for her. Most of the time, it seems to work pretty well, I guess. The youngsters know what's expected of 'em, they all live pretty much the same way of life, they've got their families all around them. But Iphigenia — oh, she liked her bloke well enough, but she didn't love him. Not the way she loved me." His eyes were

9

abstracted, lost in thoughts of the past. "Nothing wrong with him, mind — I met him, fought alongside him, he was a good bloke. And then he disappeared and they all reckoned he must be dead."

"And is that when Iphigenia turned to you?" Alix asked softly.

"No, we hadn't even met then. It was a bit later, when the evacuation was on and I got left behind — hurt my ankle climbing down the cliffs, thought I'd been left for dead until Iphigenia's brother found me. He got some of his mates and they carried me up to an old ruined monastery. They hid me in one of the rooms and the whole village took a turn at looking after me. Iphigenia came on the third day." He gave Alix a crooked, half-embarrassed grin. "I reckon we both knew, the minute we laid eyes on each other."

"Love at first sight?" she queried lightly, and her green eyes softened when he nodded. Quickly, she leaned forward and laid her small hand over his, wrinkled and knobbly with his disease. "And you've remembered her all these years."

"That's right. Mind you, I've had a good life," he added quickly. "Your grandma was a good wife to me and I loved her — don't think I didn't. We were happy together. We'd known each other as kids, grown up in and out of each other's homes — we fitted in fine together. But I never went out with her until two years after the war, when I'd finally given up on hearing from Iphigenia. Like I told you, we'd agreed she should be the one to make contact, just in case her bloke did come back. I didn't want to cause her any trouble by arriving on the scene when she was going through with this marriage. And she'd have had to do that, y'see. They take betrothals seriously on Crete and I didn't want to get mixed up in a vendetta. It would have split her family in two, something like that."

It sounded almost medieval to Alix, but she knew her grandfather was right. Even in the nineties, there was still this touch of traditional strictness amongst the people of Crete, and he was talking about fifty years ago.

"But I often wondered what she thought," he went on. "Why she didn't write — what life's been like for her since. What it's like now . . ." He looked at Alix, and then waved a hand around at his surroundings — the garden, brilliant with flowers, the house behind them. "I've got all I need here, and more. I wouldn't like to think of her in want, while I live in luxury. They live pretty poor on Crete, some of 'em."

And so Alix had agreed to come to Crete as soon as possible after her return to England, to try to find Iphigenia and to let her know that the tall, smiling young New Zealander in the photograph had never forgotten her, that thousands of miles away on the other side of the world he thought of her still. And, if she needed help of any kind, to tell her it was there for the asking.

She had fixed the trip almost as soon as she had come back to England. There was no need to go back to the *Science Today* offices yet, for her long leave of absence still had a month to run, but she'd popped in anyway to see her boss, John Kitchener, and the rest of the staff. She'd kept in touch via the Internet while in New Zealand, and sent several articles, and John grinned at her and suggested she also look out for interesting items on Crete.

Alix had shaken her head. "No way. I shan't be taking my modem with me. I don't expect to be near a telephone."

"You mean there are still places where they don't have telephones?" he asked in mock horror. "Can't you use your mobile?"

But she'd laughed at him and told him it was a holiday. Though if she found Iphigenia, she thought, her story would be far more fascinating than any of the science items she'd e-mailed through from New Zealand. But this would not be a story for publication. This story, whatever it turned out to be, was intensely private.

"Hi." A pleasant voice interrupted her thoughts and she looked up to see a man smiling down at her. He had very blue eyes and blond hair that waved smoothly back from his wide brow. His teeth looked almost impossibly white and his face was just craggy enough to crinkle attractively as he smiled. "I think this is my seat. It looks as if we're going to be travelling companions." He settled down beside her, giving her another friendly smile. "We've got a good day for the flight."

Alix nodded, feeling slightly breathless. It wasn't that she was affected by his good looks — more that this was the effect any man had on her these days. She frowned a little, feeling cross with herself. I ought to have got over all that by now, she thought. Wasn't that what the trip to New Zealand was all about?

The man held out his right hand. "My name's Gil," he said with an odd little grin to which Alix didn't know quite how to respond. "And yours?"

"Alix." Since he hadn't seen fit to tell her his surname, she didn't see any reason to tell him hers. Anyway, that was the normal thing with holiday acquaintanceships — Christian names only, and then you knew there was no commitment, no expectations. Ships that passed in the night.

Gil nodded towards the papers still in her lap. "That looks interesting."

"Just a few family photos," she said, gathering them together quickly. She didn't want to recount her grandfather's story to everyone she met. But as she did so, a child in the seat behind suddenly kicked the back of the seat and the papers slipped from her hand. Gil bent quickly to help her retrieve them. He glanced at the sketch of Iphigenia and gave a low whistle of admiration.

"She's quite a beauty. A relative of yours?"

"Not exactly." Alix held out her hand for the sketch but he was still gazing at it. As their fingers touched, a shadow fell across them and they both looked up.

The aisle was almost clear now, most of the passengers settled in their seats. There was just one man still making his way along the plane, and he had paused beside them and stood staring down. Alix met his eyes and felt her heart give a strange lurch.

I've seen you before, she thought. I *know* you. And then she shook her head impatiently. Of course she didn't know him. It was just her ridiculous memory for faces — sometimes refusing to recognise people she had met, not once but several times, at others claiming intimate acquaintance with people she had never seen before in her life. It was the curse of her life and always landing her in trouble, principally with friends who objected to being passed in the street as if they were not there. But there was nothing she could do about it. She'd tried every trick there was, had even taken courses in memory training, and nothing had ever made any difference.

She glanced up once more. The man was still staring at her, and once again she had that disconcerting sensation of something plucking at the strings of her memory. But no — she did *not* know him. There was surely no way on earth that she could have forgotten *this* face.

He was at least six feet tall, probably aged

about thirty-five, dressed casually in light grey trousers with a blue shirt open at the neck, revealing a hint of dark hair. The eyes that stared into hers were dark, almost liquid, with a shimmer of bronze encircling the wide black pupils. His head was covered with thick, curling hair the colour of a peat loch under a summer sky; his body was lean yet muscled, his bare arms strong and covered with silky black hair . . .

Alix shook herself irritably. For heaven's sake, how could she know the hair on his arms felt silky to the touch? And why was she so riveted by the sight anyway? She'd seen plenty of masculine arms, plenty of hairy chests, plenty of dark, liquid eyes. You only had to go to any beach to see them being shown off by their strutting owners. Any Greek restaurant . . . Again, she felt that soft twang on her memory.

And that's all it is, she told herself triumphantly. He's a Greek, and he looks like any one of a hundred Greek waiters. It's no more than that.

The moment had passed. She held out her hand again for the sketch and Gil handed it over to her.

"She really is a beauty, there's no doubt about it. A Cretan through and through. There's something special about them, don't you agree?" He smiled that attractive, crinkling smile again and Alix returned it rather perfunctorily as she stowed the sketch and photographs safely away in her bag. She was still feeling shaken by that brief eye-to-eye encounter with the tall Greek.

He had passed on along the aisle now, she noted with relief, and the captain was announcing the details of take-off. Alix settled back, prepared to enjoy the journey. Flying was something she'd always loved, and flying to a new place never failed to carry its own special excitement.

The trip passed without incident. Gil proved a pleasant travelling companion, ready to chat as they ate their in-flight meal, but equally ready to absorb himself in a book, leaving Alix free to gaze out of the window. He gave her no further details about himself and asked her for none.

Alix was thankful for that. As she'd told herself when she was with John Kitchener, the story of her grandfather and Iphigenia was not for public enjoyment. It was a very private story, and she knew only her grandfather's side of it. Iphigenia had her own story, which was part of her life on Crete, and Alix had no intention of disturbing it. She would, she knew, have to ask questions in order to find her, but she hoped to keep her quest discreet.

The aircraft was approaching the island. It circled overhead, swooping low over the dinosaur shape of the smaller island that lay off the main coast. Alix gazed down, hearing the chatter and comments of the other passengers.

"Always an exciting moment, arriving in a new

place," Gil's voice said in her ear, and she nodded.

The aircraft was descending now and landed with a slight bump. It taxied to a stop and there was the usual pause before the doors were opened and passengers began to file along the aisles, eager for their first glimpse of their destination.

As she came out through the door and began to descend, Alix stopped, almost knocked over by the aroma of herbs. She looked about her, bemused. Gil, who was just in front of her, turned and grinned.

"Do they spray the air? I've never smelt anything so strong."

Alix shook her head. "I think every tiny patch of earth is smothered with thyme and sage and rosemary. It's like a gigantic herb garden."

Someone bumped against her and she apologised and moved on, still staring at the blue sky, the green hills behind the small airport, the old stone buildings of Heraklion visible to her right. She wondered if this was what her grandfather had seen, all those years ago. And if the village where Iphigenia had lived was still as small, unspoilt by trippers, filled with the same aromatic scent of herbs.

Would Iphigenia herself still be there?

Her light blue cotton jacket swung in a sudden breeze and she shivered as if cold fingers had just brushed across her skin. Hastily, aware of the people behind her, she descended to the bottom

17

of the steps and turned to smile a second apology at the person who had bumped into her.

"Sorry — I was just bowled over by the scent. It's wonderful."

Her voice faded as she saw who it was and she felt again the impact of those compelling eyes. Her legs were suddenly weak and she grabbed the rail to steady herself.

The man stared at her for a moment. His black brows were drawn together in a frown and once again Alix felt a strange quiver of recognition. *Had* they met before? But she'd only been back in England for a fortnight, and had spent most of that time at home with her mother, telling her all about the trip to New Zealand and making plans for this hasty journey to Crete. She hadn't had time or opportunity to meet tall, handsome Greeks.

Not that she'd have wanted to anyway! Even after the therapy of three months in New Zealand, visiting her grandfather and touring the two islands, she was still feeling bruised over Rick. At twenty-five, with one youthful love affair behind her and one experience of being jilted almost at the altar, men were quite definitely off her agenda.

The man muttered something and Alix turned away, feeling oddly shaken and grateful that she hadn't had to sit next to him on the plane. Almost three hours in the confined space of an aircraft seat, pressed close to that extremely male presence, would have been a bit too much to endure. And I bet he's the sort who wants to put his elbows on *both* arm-rests! she thought, brushing back her short cap of chestnut hair and following the rest of the passengers into the terminal building.

The luggage came through quickly and within half an hour Alix and the rest of the passengers who had booked with her tour operator were sitting on a coach, waiting to be taken on to the Rethymnon region. Gil had moved away with a slightly regretful smile of farewell, and to her relief, the tall Greek was not amongst them either, but as the coach moved out to the road she caught sight of him striding across the tarmac towards a large, glossy car. A plump, middle-aged woman was standing beside it, and she ran forwards and flung herself into his arms, her face alight with pleasure. She was joined by a stout man who got out of the car and came to give his own exuberant greeting, and they were still standing together, laughing and embracing each other, as the coach turned towards Heraklion and Alix lost sight of them.

Well, there are three people satisfied, she thought, shrugging, but she was conscious of a pang of misery somewhere deep inside. Everywhere she looked, it seemed that she saw either families or couples, walking hand in hand, talking and eating together, greeting or sometimes parting. And even that can't be so bad, she thought, if you know you're going to be together again. If you know there's someone

19

waiting for you, missing you . . .

No. She would not let her thoughts turn in that direction again. She'd spent enough time burning over Rick, wondering why he had left her, why at the last moment he had decided he couldn't go through with their wedding. He hadn't been able to explain it then and she had to accept the fact that he probably never would. And there was no point in wasting any more time over it.

But if only I *knew*, she argued for the thousandth time. If it was something wrong with me, something that makes men leave me, I might have a chance to put it right. It's not *fair* to say you love someone and then to leave them without even saying why! It leaves them unfinished. And how can anyone go on to something new when the old thing is still unfinished?

Not that I want to go on to anything new, she reminded herself. Not in the way of men, anyway. There's a whole world out there waiting for me, a world where a woman doesn't have to have a man any more, where women can have careers and single lives, and do whatever they want to do, where they don't have to give up their lives and take second place to a man's career, or spend their days drudging at a kitchen sink and slaving for a family who will only grow up and leave them. I ought to be thanking Rick on my bended knees for saving me from such a fate!

Determined not to let him occupy any more of

her thoughts, she turned her mind to the task of finding Iphigenia. How easy would it be? she wondered, gazing out at the geraniums and broom which splashed the main road to Rethymnon with colour. If she simply walked into the little village of Sellia, straggled along its ledge on the cliffs above the southern shore of the island, and asked the first person she met to direct her to Iphigenia's house, would she be talking to the old woman within the next few minutes? Or would she be met by blank stares and shakes of the head? Told that Iphigenia had moved away? Or died?

Sadly, she acknowledged to herself that this was the most likely answer. The girl Ian McConnell had loved could have been no more than two or three years younger than he. She would be over seventy now. And had lived a hard life. *'They live pretty poor on Crete, some of 'em,'* her grandfather had said.

Well, soon she would find out. And as she looked again at the sketch and the photograph, she realised that this mission meant more to her than she had first supposed.

She had accepted it because it was important to her grandfather. It was something she could do for the old man, something that would take the last little cloud of anxiety from his blue eyes. Iphigenia had haunted his mind for too long. If he knew what had happened to her — if he knew that she had been happy — he could spend his last years in contentment.

Alix prayed that she had been happy.

At first, that had been Alix's only reason for agreeing to his request. But now, she knew that there was more. Finding Iphigenia, tying up these last loose ends in her grandfather's life, enabling him to finish in his mind something that had been left undecided for fifty years — this would somehow help her come to terms with her own 'unfinished business'. It would help her finally to come to terms with Rick's desertion and take up the threads of her own life.

The coach was running into Rethymnon and Alix looked out at a mixture of old buildings and new — a fantastic juxtaposition of ancient Cretan stonework and modern concrete. She saw the bastions of the old fort standing out against the shoreline, the gleaming azure of the bay stretching beyond, with its glittering waters alive with dancing sailing craft, and she made up her mind that when she had completed her task she would come back here to explore the old city.

The coach stopped only briefly, for most of the passengers were bound for the southern part of the region, and Alix gazed out with interest as they turned inland towards the mountains that strode along the central spine from east to west. The road was still good, rising towards the pass that would take them through the *massif*, and she was fascinated by the steep slopes so densely clothed in foliage and the scatter of villages, huddled in the folds. There were flowers everywhere — geraniums mounded like scarlet cushions, huge swathes of golden broom, wild gladioli like brave, fluttering flags, their brilliant colours almost vibrating in the still, warm air. Alix felt a sudden glow of pleasure in the fact that she had, through spending the winter months in New Zealand and enjoying the best of the weather there, come to Crete in spring, when the countryside was at its best.

The coach had come over the top of the pass now and took a sudden dive into a deep, narrow gorge. With the rest of the passengers, Alix caught her breath, gazing up to either side at the towering cliffs, ducking involuntarily as the coach passed under a wide overhang, peering down at the drop on the left-hand side, where a river ran far below on its way to the sea.

"You'll see the shrines set at the side of the road," the courier remarked, and they all strained their necks to look. "They're in memory of people who drove off the road at these points!" The passengers recoiled, sitting back in their seats and laughing nervously. "It's all right," she went on reassuringly, "none of them were in coaches. Our drivers take far better care of you than that."

A few moments later they came out into the sunshine and everyone gasped again at the view. The whole of Plakias Bay lay spread out before them, with the shore curving round like a horseshoe to contain the shimmering blue waves, and silvery-green olive groves running down to white sands.

Plakias itself, Alix knew, was clustered at one end of the bay, with the old villages like Sellia on the cliffs above. All the old Cretan villages were on the cliffs, or inland a little, for the population had suffered heavily in the past from pirates. Now the only invaders were the tourists who wanted to be close to the beach, so the new village had grown up around the tiny fishing harbour, a tangle of small hotels and apartments, with a character of its own.

The coach drew up at the small apartment block where Alix was staying. She was the only passenger to alight, and she stood on the roadside feeling a little lonely, watching the rest depart to their hotels. Most of them had looked pleasant and friendly and she wondered if she would see them again — perhaps in one of the tavernas where she would go for her evening meals.

The apartment block was an older one, smaller than most, built in traditional style and surrounded by a grove of gnarled and twisted olive trees. Alix stood for a few moments outside, breathing in the scented air and revelling in the gentle warmth of the sun on her bare arms. A door opened and closed behind her and she turned to see a stocky Greek approach, his dark face wreathed in smiles.

"Miss Berringer?" He spoke good English, not too heavily accented to understand, and Alix smiled at him with some relief. "Your room is ready for you. I'll carry your bag."

Alix followed him. Her apartment was small but clean and adequate, with a minute kitchen, shower and bedroom. It was on the ground floor and had its own tiny garden space, with an olive tree for shade and a view of the bay. She dropped her bags on the bed and looked around with pleasure.

"It's lovely. Thank you very much."

He inclined his head. "You are welcome. I am sorry we do not provide meals here, but there are plenty of tavernas in the village. And breakfast will be brought to your room whenever you wish. I will bring it myself."

She smiled at him. He spoke proudly, not with the obsequiousness of a man who thinks himself too good to serve, but with the confidence of one who knows he does his job well. The pride of a Cretan, who does nothing that he does not consider befits him.

He left her and she turned to gaze out again over the view of the bay. Well, even if she did not find Iphigenia, it would be no hardship to spend a week or two in this pleasant place. And if it helped her to thrust Rick finally from her mind, so that she could go back to London and take up the threads of her life again . . .

That was what the trip to New Zealand was supposed to do, she thought ruefully. And much as I enjoyed it, he's still there, getting in my way. Can two weeks on a Greek island do what three months in New Zealand couldn't?

It all depended on whether she could find

Iphigenia. And on what the Cretan woman's life had been like in the half-century since she had fallen in love with a smiling young New Zealand soldier.

Chapter Two

There were only a few tavernas open in the village, for it was still early in the season and the tourists had not yet arrived in any great numbers. Refreshed by a warm shower and wearing a brightly coloured silk skirt and lacy white blouse, Alix wandered through the village, pausing to look in the few shop windows — mostly grocery stores and small supermarkets — and leaned over the bridge which crossed a small stream, to try to spot the toads she could hear croaking in the twilight.

There was a taverna beside the bridge, with most of its patio tables already occupied. She hesitated for a moment, then went inside. A plump, smiling woman showed her to a small table in a corner, and beckoned to a young waiter in jeans and white shirt, who threaded his way through the tables and asked if she would like a drink. Alix ordered a small carafe of wine and accepted some bread, then studied the menu written up on a large blackboard fixed to the wall.

The restaurant seemed to be one large room, the dining area divided from the kitchen only by a long counter on which the meals were placed when ready to be collected by the waiters and waitresses. Behind it the kitchen staff were working like beavers, stirring steaming pans on the big stove, mixing and beating things in bowls at the long tables, chopping vegetables and herbs or cleaning fish and meat at the wide sink. Clearly, all the food was prepared fresh and to order, and everything orchestrated by the tall chef, whose white hat seemed almost to touch the ceiling as he oversaw the preparations.

Alix watched him thoughtfully. His face was hidden from her but there was something familiar in his bearing and once again she felt a flicker of awareness at the edge of her mind. Then he turned and glanced across the counter into the restaurant. Their eyes met and she felt a jolt of recognition.

It was him again. The man who had stared at her in the aeroplane, who had bumped into her on the steps. So he was a chef, perhaps even the owner of the taverna. But that didn't explain why he should have stopped what he was doing to come round the dividing counter and make his way to her table . . .

Alix stared at him, her heart bumping uncomfortably. Although she had recognised him, there was still an uneasy sensation in her mind that she had known him before today. In another life, perhaps? she thought wildly, and scorned the notion. Of course she had never seen him before. Even if she had, he had played no part in her life. He simply looks like someone I know, she thought, or like someone I've seen on TV.

But why was he coming over to her table?

He stopped in front of her and she looked up at him, feeling almost intimidated by the power that emanated from him. It's just an impression, because he's so big, she thought — not real power at all. Yet he wasn't bulky — his broad shoulders were perfectly in proportion with his height, and even under his white apron it could be seen that they narrowed down to a lean waist and small buttocks. Perhaps it wasn't so much size — when you were only five foot three you grew used to feeling smaller than everyone else — but actual power, after all. Sheer, confident, *male* power.

The sort of power that could present a real threat.

At that thought, every defence mechanism in her body swung into action. Ridiculous — what threat could a Greek chef hold for her? But ever since Rick, this had been her reaction to any man who came a little too close for comfort. She'd been too badly hurt to want it to happen again, and as soon as her body recognised the signals of masculinity it responded by putting up the barriers.

"Yes?" she said coolly, meeting his eyes.

"Everything is to your satisfaction?" he enquired, and she glanced at the table before answering. There was nothing on it but the bread basket.

29

"I can't tell you yet," she said politely. "I haven't even ordered."

"Perhaps I can recommend something." His English was extremely good, almost without accent. "The moussaka — that's a traditional Greek dish you might enjoy. Minced lamb with aubergine —"

"Thank you. I know what moussaka is." Then, thinking she might have sounded rude, she added quickly, "I like it very much. Yes please, I'll have the moussaka."

He looked a little disappointed, as if he had wanted to recite the whole menu for her. Then he said, "We have met before."

"I remember," Alix said briefly. "On the plane."

His eyes were very dark. They regarded her thoughtfully, as if he were about to say something else. She recalled her earlier feeling of having seen him before and dismissed it. He's just trying to chat me up! she thought indignantly.

"If I could have my dinner?" she suggested stonily. "I *am* rather hungry."

His face changed, his expression cooling a little, then he made a slight bow and said, "Of course. I'm afraid that on Crete we tend to think that there is plenty of time in the world for sitting over a meal, watching the sun go down over the sea. You will have to forgive us if we don't have the efficiency you are accustomed to in London."

He turned and strode quickly back to the kitchen, leaving Alix gasping. His words had been spoken in a perfectly polite, if clipped, voice, but it was clear she'd annoyed him. But why? What had he expected? Should she have greeted him like a long-lost friend, simply because he'd bumped into her on the steps of the plane? Was she supposed to fall for his masculine charms?

That was probably it. Alix remembered the countless stories of Spanish and Greek waiters, preying on English girls holidaying abroad. And what about *Shirley Valentine*? The next thing would be an offer to take her out in his fishing-boat!

With a shrug, she dismissed him from her mind and settled down to watch the comings and goings around her, smiling at the fat little German toddler who was staggering between the tables, and trying not to look with envy at the couples who sat holding hands or smiling into each other's eyes.

I could have been part of such a couple, she thought. If only Rick hadn't . . . and then she caught herself up. Such thoughts were definitely not allowed.

Get out, Rick! she told him sternly. This is *my* life now — you don't have any part of it.

But wasn't that the worst of it — that he had so clearly told her he didn't *want* any part of it? At the memory of that last scene, she felt the heat of tears in her eyes yet again, and blinked them

angrily away, Get *out*, Rick . . .

"Hi. D'you mind if I join you?"

Alix glanced up, startled. Surely it couldn't be the chef again, arrogantly certain of his welcome. But instead she found herself looking up into the blue, smiling eyes of the man she had sat next to on the plane — Gil.

"Oh —" she said, momentarily confused. "Oh, no, of course not. Please —"

Gil sat down opposite her and she studied him covertly. His hair was the colour of ripe corn and his eyes very blue and smiling. He had an air of self-confidence about him, almost as if he expected her to recognise him, and she wondered if he might be an actor. But she had seen almost no television or films in the past two years or so, for her job had kept her busy, plus preparing for her wedding — the wedding that never was! she thought wryly — and in New Zealand her grandfather's television had stayed mostly mute in a corner.

"You weren't waiting for anyone else, were you?" he asked. "I wouldn't want to intrude . . . And if you'd rather be by yourself, do say so." He smiled charmingly, rather like a very well-brought-up little boy. "But if you're alone — and I'm alone — well, it might be rather pleasant to eat in company, don't you think?"

"Yes — oh, yes," Alix stammered. "Much more pleasant." Her wine arrived and she poured herself a glass, thankful for the distraction. What was the matter with her? She was behaving like a teenager out on her first date. And she wasn't even *on* a date!

"I didn't think I'd see you in a tiny place like this," he observed. "Somehow, I had the impression you were bound for Heraklion."

"And I thought you were!" she confessed with a little laugh. "But I guessed you knew the island well. Have you been here many times?"

"A couple. In fact, I know the whole of Greece pretty well." He glanced around. "This is a very good little place. It's always full — you have to be here early if you want a table. *And* if you want a full choice from the menu — they cook everything fresh, unlike a lot of tavernas, and don't buy in more than they think they'll need."

The plump woman came to the table and took his order, which he gave in Greek. There was a good deal of laughing banter between the two and when she had gone, Alix said, "I'm impressed! I don't think I could ever learn Greek."

He smiled, showing his very even, white teeth. "I told you, I've spent quite a lot of time here. It's my favourite hideaway." He gave her a glance, as if expecting some reaction to this remark, then went on, "I like the quieter spots — I get tired of crowds all the time, being in London so much. D'you live in London?"

Alix nodded. "I've lived there for several years now. I'm a science journalist."

"That sounds high-powered! And you say you couldn't learn Greek?"

33

She laughed. "Well, I managed to learn as much as I needed to." Her salad arrived and she picked up her knife and fork. "What did you order? I'm having the moussaka."

The kitchen was in full view, behind the counter, and Alix could see the waiters and waitresses hurrying back and forth with orders and meals. Clouds of steam rose from big pans set on the huge ovens and the head chef, his white hat almost touching the ceiling, was vigorously stirring something in a bowl.

"Haven't seen that chef here before," her companion said. "Yet he looks familiar. I seem to associate him with somewhere else." His blue eyes were narrowed and thoughtful.

Alix glanced at him in surprise.

"How odd — I had the same feeling. He must have a lookalike somewhere."

"Mm, perhaps." Gil gazed across the counter. "But it's more than that. I'll remember in a minute — I seldom forget a face." He thought for a few moments. "Yes, I've got it — he looks like the owner of a Greek restaurant I go to quite a lot in London. The Minos. I don't suppose you know it?"

"Near Covent Garden?" Alix stared at him. "Yes, I know it quite well — I used to go there a lot myself." She remembered the last time she had been there, and her mind turned abruptly away from the memory. "I — haven't been for quite a few months, though."

"Oh? Didn't you like the food?"

34

Alix laughed, relieved to be able to give him a good reason for not having been to the Minos lately. "No, I've been abroad. In New Zealand. I went to visit my grandfather." She looked again at the chef, wanting to get away from a discussion of her personal life. "You're right, he does look like the owner. Maybe they're brothers . . ." Her voice faded away.

Gil glanced at her curiously. "What is it? You look as if you've just seen a ghost."

With an effort, Alix pulled herself together and smiled. "No, no ghosts — I'm fine. Just a goose walking over my grave . . . What a horrid expression that is," she went on, making her voice light. "And why should a goose have that effect anyway? I've never even *seen* a goose in a grave-yard, have you?" She was chattering, but did it matter? She and Gil were just chance acquaintances, they would probably never even see each other again. Keep it light, she thought, keep the evening flowing, eat your meal and chatter and then go back to the apartment and go to sleep. And tomorrow you can do what you came here to do, you can go to Sellia and find Iphigenia.

And forget that last evening with Rick. Forget the tall Greek and his dark, unsmiling eyes, who had bumped into her on the aircraft steps earlier that afternoon.

Who just might be the owner of a restaurant called the Minos in London, near Covent Garden and, if so, had witnessed everything on that last, humiliating evening . . .

35

There had been no hint in Rick's manner that he was about to bring her whole world crashing down about her ears. No touch of coolness, no reserve as he collected her from her flat and drove with his usual expertise through the London streets to the Minos. His smile had been as warm as ever, his touch on her arm as lightly caressing. And if afterwards, reliving every moment, she thought that there might perhaps have been just a little less passion than usual in his kiss when they first said hello, it was barely detectable and could easily have been no more than the knowledge of hindsight. Because by then it had happened. By then, her world had tumbled.

They had chosen moussaka. It was always especially good here, cooked by the proprietor himself. He'd welcomed them to their usual table, giving Alix the dark, liquid glance that always made her shiver a little inside. If she hadn't been with Rick . . . But she always was with Rick, or with someone like her boss, John Kitchener, or one of the authors she sometimes took to lunch. And she wasn't in the market for being chatted up by Greek waiters anyway.

Not that this man would have been flattered to have thought himself dismissed as a waiter, she thought. He carried himself with the proud bearing of a king, and his staff treated him as if he were indeed regal. They obviously worshipped him.

Perhaps, Alix considered afterwards, it was

because she had been so preoccupied with wedding plans that she had noticed nothing unusual in his manner. Perhaps she ought to have paid him more attention instead of being so blissfully wrapped up in the preparations — the decisions to be made over bridesmaids' dresses, the question of lace or brocade for her own gown, the decorations of the flat they were buying together.

There must have been signs. There must have been moments when Rick's enthusiasm could have been seen to be waning. There must have been *some* warning, some little hint that could have saved her the anguish of that terrible, bald announcement.

But try though she might during the long, lonely nights that followed, the hours of darkness which she should have been spending in Rick's arms, Alix could think of nothing. And that had shattered her confidence even more. How could she ever trust her own judgement again? she wondered. How could she ever offer a man her love, knowing how blind she could be?

The moussaka had arrived, and had proved as delicious as usual. Afterwards, Rick had declined a dessert but Alix had fallen to temptation as usual and ordered a honey-sweet cake, smothered with nuts, to eat with her coffee. And it was then that he'd dropped his bombshell.

"Alix," he said, interrupting her conjectures about bridesmaids' dresses and lampshades. "Alix, I've got something to tell you."

She stopped speaking at once, aware of the seriousness of his voice, and stared at him. "What? What is it?"

He met her eyes for a moment. Then his glance dropped away. He stared at a tiny crumb on the table and put his fingertip on it.

"It isn't easy —"

"Rick, what is it?" Her voice rose in alarm. "What's happened? Is it your job — you haven't lost your job, have you?"

He looked startled. "My job?" Rick was a consultant with an advertising agency. "No, of course I haven't lost my job." He sounded slightly nettled at the very suggestion. "It's nothing to do with my job. Alix —"

"Tell me," she broke in. She was filled with sudden, unreasoning panic. "Rick, for God's sake stop fiddling with that crumb and *tell me!*"

He glanced at her again. "Calm down, Alix." He took his finger off the crumb and laid his hand on hers. "Look, it isn't easy so you'll just have to let me tell you in my own time and my own way." He took a deep breath. "It's about our wedding —"

"Our . . . *wedding?*"

"Alix — please." He stopped for a moment. "Oh, hell — there isn't any easy way. There isn't even a kind way." He took another deep breath, while Alix stared at him, fighting the rising wave of fear. "I'm sorry, Alix, I can't marry you. It's off."

There was a long, long silence. To Alix, it

seemed as if the whole restaurant was suddenly still. She stared at his face, into his shuttered eyes, and then looked away, unable to bear it. She looked slowly around her, at the other diners, at the tall Greek who owned the restaurant, standing at the far end, watching — watching *her,* she thought wildly — and then back at Rick. She hoped it had been a mistake, that when she looked at his face again she would see the love and laughter she'd always found there. But there was nothing.

Only that shut-away look. As if the Rick she knew and loved was no longer there.

"Alix," he said, "I'm sorry."

"Sorry?" she said carefully, as if it were a word she'd never heard before. "Sorry?" And then, with a surge of emotion composed partly of disbelief, partly of anguish, partly of anger that he should do this to her, that he should let her get so far, build such hopes — and that he should choose this place of all places to do it, "You're *sorry?* Is that all you can say?" She stared at him, feeling the sensations rush back as pain rushes back into a cramped limb. "You calmly smash my life — all our hopes and plans, all we've talked about and worked for — and sit there and say you're *sorry?*" She shook her head, blinking back sudden tears. "Why? What's happened to change your mind? What have I done?"

"Nothing. It's nothing you've done." He shrugged helplessly. "I can't tell you why, Alix. I just know I can't go through with it, that's all."

"That's all," she echoed in a whisper. "That's all. Everything I've thought about for the past six months thrown away, and you say *that's all*. Well, it's not all for me. It's not *enough* for me." She lifted the half-full carafe of wine from the table and held it high, inwardly exulting at the look of alarm on his face.

"Alix — for God's sake, don't make a scene here —"

"*Me* not make a scene?" she repeated. "I might remind you, Rick, that *you* caused this. You chose to tell me our wedding was off — and you chose the place to do it. And all you can say is you're sorry. Well, I'm sorry too, Rick — sorry I ever let myself fall in love with you. And this is *my* choice of a reply."

She emptied the carafe over his head. The wine fell in a graceful cascade, spattering on his hair and shoulders. Alix heard a gasp from the nearby tables and was briefly aware of the Greek proprietor striding towards them. Then she burst into tears and ran out of the restaurant.

Chapter Three

By seven-thirty next morning, Alix was up, and eating her breakfast beneath the olive tree outside her apartment. The owner had kept his promise and had provided her with warm rolls, she had bought fruit from the little supermarket by the beach, and the aroma of fresh coffee wafted out through the open door. A pair of goldfinches twittered in the branches of the tree, and out on the bay a drift of thin mist lay like chiffon on the calm blue water.

She spread her grandfather's papers out on the table before her and studied them again. Here was the photograph, the laughing face still recognizable as the old New Zealander she had visited three months before, even though they were separated by half a century. The old map of the bay, hand-drawn, that he had been given by Iphigenia's brother all that time ago. A sketch of the house the family lived in, drawn from memory, and the sketch of Iphigenia herself, looking out of the picture with an expression of such love and tenderness that it never failed to catch at Alix's heart. She stared at it again, wondering — as her grandfather had done — just what had happened to the Cretan girl, and what she had felt when she had realised at last that she would never see her lover again.

'We'd agreed she should be the one to make contact,' Ian McConnell had said. But she never had. What had prevented her? Had she tried — written a letter which had never reached him, perhaps? Had she waited for him, hoping that he would come? Had she gazed out over the bay where he had disappeared in that last submarine, yearning for him to return? Had she, too, felt the pain of desertion?

With a swift, abrupt movement, Alix swept the papers together and thrust them into her bag. She got up and carried her breakfast things indoors, put on her walking boots and pushed another roll, some cheese and a huge tomato into her small rucksack. With the rest of the fruit, that would be enough to sustain her through the day, and there would surely be tavernas if she needed anything else. She locked the apartment door behind her and set off up the narrow road through the olive grove.

Nobody else was about. The road was little more than a track, winding up the hill. The morning sun slanted down through the silvery trees and, ahead of her, small birds fluttered away into the branches. The air reverberated with birdsong, the grass beneath the olives patched with the sunshine yellow of sorrel in flower. The coolness of the morning was already blending into the warmth of day, and she took off her light jacket and felt the air brush against her bare arms like warm feathers. How hot would it be later on? she wondered, thinking that it might have been better to wear shorts rather than the slim, dark blue cotton trousers she had put on. But shorts weren't recommended for Crete: the foliage on the hills and footpaths could be prickly, and wearing them into the little churches that abounded in every valley might cause offence.

Alix had been walking fast. Now she slowed her steps. What was the hurry? It was still before nine on her first morning here. She had a week — two, if she wanted to stay — to find Iphigenia and talk to her about her grandfather and days gone by. And it surely wouldn't be that difficult to find her. Crete was a large island but it was populated mainly by people who lived in small, close-knit communities. Even if Iphigenia had moved away from Sellia, someone there would know where she was and how to contact her.

All the same, she needed to be careful. She remembered her grandfather's warnings about the rigid family structures on Crete. Betrothals and marriages were taken very seriously indeed, and any infringement could spark off trouble — feuds that could last for generations, vendettas that sometimes resulted in tragedy. Even if Iphigenia had married half a century before, her life could be ruined by a thoughtless intervention from the past.

Once again Alix found her mind invaded by a picture of the Greek who had bumped into her on the plane, who had turned out to be the chef in the taverna last night and who looked so much like the owner of the restaurant in London. Could it possibly be the same man? Could co-incidence stretch so far? But need it necessarily be much of a coincidence? she wondered. Chefs could travel, just like anyone else, and the number of planes coming from London to Crete were limited. Or was he a relative — a brother, perhaps? It wasn't so unreasonable for a Cretan who owned a taverna here to have a brother running a similar business in London.

It really is a pity I don't have a better memory for faces, she thought. Half the time she couldn't even recall the names of regular acquaintances. Her chances of remembering for certain the proprietor of a Greek restaurant in London, whom she couldn't have seen for several months and then only in a dim light, were slim indeed.

And why did it matter anyway? He was nothing more than an opportunist, who had noticed a young woman sitting alone and decided to make a play for her. She smiled, thinking of Gil who had sat chatting until long after the meal had ended. That ought to have made it plain to the Greek that his attentions were unwelcome. She realised, a little guiltily, that this was the only reason she had encouraged the tall, blond Englishman — but why not, after all? He'd been only normally friendly, not in the least importunate, and the evening had passed swiftly and pleasantly. They had parted with the vague expectation of meeting again — holiday acquaintances, ships that passed in the night, and no more than that.

The Greek hadn't thought so, though, she reflected, recalling his dark eyes watching them over the dividing counter. He had seen Gil come to the table and sit down, and almost certainly assumed they were together. And that was all to the good. If there was one thing Alix didn't need during her stay in Crete, it was having to evade pursuit by a Greek taverna owner who had seen *Shirley Valentine* and thought all lone female visitors were easy prey.

Alix came out of the olive grove and looked up the steep little path that wound its way up to the village above. A donkey was tethered at the side of the road, a wooden saddle on the grass beside it. It stopped cropping the grass and regarded her with mild brown eyes, its long ears pricking forward as she spoke to it. On the track above, an old woman was walking slowly behind a small flock of sheep and goats, their bells tinkling like the music of a cascade as they skipped around her full black skirts.

She tried to picture the Greek restaurateur she had known in London. The Minos was near the *Science Today* office, and she had frequently taken science writers there for lunch. But it was also handy for many of the London theatres and she and Rick had been in the habit of dropping in for a meal after seeing a show. She had known several of the waiters by name, and usually

exchanged a word or two with the proprietor —
who, she was becoming more and more certain,
bore an uncannily strong resemblance to the
chef she had met last night.

But how *could* he be running a restaurant in
London, and at the same time be working in a
small taverna in Plakias?

And what did it matter? He was nothing to
her, never would be anything to her. So why did
she feel such a sense of unease when he was near
her — as if he were a danger to her peace of
mind?

The houses of Sellia were dazzlingly white in
the brilliant sunshine, and the little onion-
domed church looked as if it had been scrubbed
and polished that very morning. Indeed, as Alix
gazed at it an old woman, wearing a long black
dress and shawl, shuffled out of the door carrying a bucket and mop. She passed Alix and
gave her a toothless smile before continuing on
her way along the village street.

Bother! Alix thought, watching her disappear
through a doorway. I ought to have asked her
about Iphigenia. But would she have understood
me if I had? Do the older people speak English?
Perhaps I ought to look for someone younger.

Easier said than done, she thought a few
moments later as she wandered along the street.
Nearly everyone here appeared to be the other
side of sixty, if not seventy or eighty. Or perhaps
people in the Mediterranean countries simply

looked older than they were? Whatever the answer, none of them seemed to understand much English. They nodded and smiled at her, returned her greetings, but looked blank when she began to question them.

There was a small taverna, already open and patronised by a group of men, some of them no more than middle-aged. They looked at her appreciatively as she paused in the doorway. She gave them a quick smile and produced her sketch of Iphigenia.

The men craned forward to stare at it and their faces cracked into even more appreciative smiles. One of them said something which made the others laugh. Alix felt her face burn and snatched the picture away, wishing she had not displayed it at all, and then was immediately ashamed when the men stared at her in surprise.

They didn't mean any offence, she thought, and it was pointless to antagonise them at this stage. How could she expect them to help her? She looked from one to the other and asked, "Does anyone speak English?"

Their faces lit up again and one man shifted his chair forward a little. He tapped his chest proudly.

"I speak English, yes. You look for a room?"

Alix shook her head. "Not a room, no. I'm staying in Plakias —"

At this, there was a chorus of voices. From the few English words that escaped the babble, and from the general tone of the chorus, Alix gathered that she would be very much better off staying in Sellia, and that any one of the men in the taverna was willing — no, *eager* — to offer her accommodation. There was much jostling and laughter, and the owner of the taverna came over with a tray of small glasses, insisting that Alix take one and drink a toast — though to what, she had no idea.

The liquid was like firewater, with a sharp taste of aniseed. Presumably, she thought, feeling her eyes begin to water, it was ouzo. The men were watching her now as she swallowed, blinked a little, and smiled her thanks. Then she looked again at the English-speaker.

"I really don't want a room — I like to be near the sea. But I'm looking for someone — someone who used to live in Sellia." She touched the sketch of Iphigenia. "She'll be old now — probably past seventy — but she used to look like this."

The man was staring at her, his lips moving slightly as he tried to follow her words, and she realised that he had not understood a word. Feeling suddenly helpless again, she touched the tender face her grandfather had drawn all those years ago, and said, "Iphigenia. That's her name. Do you know her?"

The men looked at each other. They were frowning, puzzled. They began to talk again, evidently discussing what she had just said, interpreting it and trying to make sense of it. At last, the man who had claimed to speak English turned back to Alix.

"Iphigenia? Young girl?"

"Not now. Old. Old woman." She wondered whether to mime the image of old age, but decided it might be offensive to the more ancient of the men sitting round the table. She gazed helplessly at the mystified faces. How could she explain? Wasn't there *anyone* in the village who spoke English?

For the first time, she began to wonder if her task was as simple as it had appeared.

I need an interpreter, she thought. Someone who can speak both languages well enough to translate my questions and their answers.

She thought of Gil, the tall Englishman with the corn-coloured hair and white smile who had shared her meal last night. He had suggested meeting again, perhaps driving somewhere together in the car he'd hired, but Alix had declined gracefully, saying that she had come for some walking. They'd parted with casual friendliness and she hadn't expected to see much more of him — nor had she especially wanted to. Pleasant though he was, she was determined not to get involved, particularly here on Crete.

All the same, she'd quite enjoyed his company at dinner. And if he could speak Greek — as he had done when ordering his dinner — maybe she could ask his help in tracking down Iphigenia.

The unfortunate thing about that was that she didn't know where he was staying — and their only point of contact was the taverna, where the

Greek who was so mysteriously and implacably hostile to her, worked as chef . . .

A shadow darkened the doorway and Alix turned hopefully. Perhaps the newcomer would be able to help. Or was it just another of the village ancients, arriving for his morning drink and gossip with his friends?

It was impossible, in the dimness of the little room, to see the newcomer's face, but he was big enough almost to fill the doorway. Not an ancient, anyway. He seemed to be staring in, his head moving slightly as he took in the scene, and she realised that he was now looking directly at her. The rest of the men were suddenly silent, almost watchful.

With a sudden unaccountable flicker of nervousness, Alix went towards him, holding out her sketch.

To her complete astonishment, he spoke in English. And his voice was unexpectedly — almost alarmingly — familiar, making the words, innocuous as they were, seem oddly intimidating.

"You seem to be having some kind of trouble. Anything I can do?"

Alix stared at him. He shifted slightly, so that the light fell on his face, and she realised with a shock that it was the Greek chef again. Instinctively she drew back, alarmed once more by the overpowering sense of masculinity that surrounded him. He seemed to wear it like a cloak, she thought, and with as much pride as a king.

The impression was increased by the behaviour of the other men. Proud as they were — for they were all Cretans, the proudest of all the Greeks — they seemed to withdraw a little in the presence of this man. As if it were natural for them to defer to him. As if he held some kind of power over them too, an authority which they recognised and to which they acquiesced.

"What's the problem?" he asked again, and then turned to the men and evidently repeated his question in Greek.

There was an instant babble of voices as everyone tried to explain at once. Though what they could be telling him, Alix thought, was a mystery since none of them had understood what she wanted. She watched him, noticing that his air of authority was completely casual, the sense of easy command appearing to exude from his pores. This was a man accustomed to taking charge, and respected by the men he was talking to now. Known to them. How could he be the man she remembered in London?

He turned back to her. "They tell me you're looking for someone. A young girl called Iphigenia." His eyes were narrowed slightly. "Would you mind telling me why?"

Alix shook her head. She still felt uneasy in his presence, but at least he could speak English and there was no reason why she shouldn't ask his help. "It's not a young girl, it's an old woman. This is a picture of her when she was young — over fifty years ago." She held out the sketch and

51

he took it and scanned it, his dark brows drawn together. "I know hardly anyone's likely to recognise her from that," she said apologetically, "but it's all I have. And someone might remember her when she was young . . ."

He glanced up and his eyes met hers. She recoiled slightly under the impact of his gaze. The liquid darkness of his eyes had hardened, like lava solidifying to rock. His face was like stone. When he spoke, there was a harsh edge to his voice.

"Why do you want to find this woman?"

Alix flinched. Feeling suddenly angry, she said curtly, "That's not something I'm prepared to discuss, other than with her. Do you know who she is?"

He didn't answer at once and she got the impression that he was turning the matter over in his mind, debating with himself what to say.

She held out her hand. "May I have my sketch back, please? If you don't know Iphigenia, per- haps you wouldn't mind telling me where I might find someone who does. She used to live in this village, there must be somebody . . . some of these men here *must* have known her then. Doesn't anyone recognise her?"

The Greek stared at her. He held the paper slightly out of her reach, and she felt her temper rise. He glanced around at the circle of intent faces, and then seemed to make up his mind.

"It's useless," he said. "There may have been someone called Iphigenia here years ago, but she's not any longer. She's gone. None of these men remember her, or know what became of her. You might as well give up and go home."

The abruptness of it took Alix's breath away. The hostility in his tone was impossible to mistake, and his glowering expression told her that any 'help' he might have offered was purely notional. He had no more intention of helping her than of sprouting wings.

Was he telling her the truth? She looked at the men and they glanced away, shifting uncomfortably in their chairs. What had happened? A moment ago, they were friendly, eager to help. Now, they refused to meet her eyes.

Once again, she recalled her grandfather's warning, and shivered. Perhaps trouble had come of his love for the Cretan girl all those years ago, trouble which still reverberated around the island. Perhaps she had stumbled already into a vendetta.

If that were so, she thought, then her task was doubly important. For what Ian McConnell wanted most of all was to know that his young sweetheart was comfortable and well cared for in her old age. If not, he wanted the chance to do something about it.

If she were still suffering under the harsh laws of vendetta, then she needed his help. And Alix could not leave the island until she knew the truth.

She faced the tall Greek and brushed back her short, tawny hair, tilting her chin to look up into

53

his face. Her green eyes sparked with the anger that injustice and arrogance always aroused in her. She spoke in her iciest voice.

"I have no intention of giving up, nor of going home until I've found Iphigenia or know what happened to her. She *did* live here — I know that — and there must be people who remember her. And I don't see why you should take it upon yourself to speak for them. It's none of your business anyway."

His eyes narrowed.

"That's for me to decide. It's certainly my business when you come here, haranguing and worrying people who are friends of mine —"

The sheer injustice of his words brought her simmering temper to flashpoint. "Worrying? Haranguing?" she flared. "I did nothing of the kind! I simply came in to ask a polite question. They were perfectly willing to help until you marched in and took over." She looked at the faces of the men, who were staring at the table or at the floor, clearly embarrassed, one or two of them actually scowling. "What have you said to them about me? What have you told them?"

"Only the truth," he said blandly, and she stared at him.

"What truth? You don't even know me — how can you know any 'truth'? We haven't even met before. You don't have any idea what I'm doing here."

"Oh, but I do," he said coolly, unruffled by her anger. "I know exactly what you're doing here.

And my advice to you is — forget it. There's nothing here for you, Miss Berringer, nothing at all."

Alix stared at him. Her skin grew cold. He did know her! He knew her name. But how? And what did he mean when he said that he knew why she was here?

Nobody but her grandfather and her mother knew why she was here.

"I don't know who you are," she said, striving to keep her voice from shaking, "or how you happen to know my name — but somehow or other you've got the wrong idea. All I want is to find Iphigenia. What's so wrong with that?"

"You know the answer to that as well as I do," he replied maddeningly. "Or — perhaps you don't. Perhaps you really don't realise the havoc that you and people like you can wreak in the lives of other people, ordinary people who just want to be left alone. In any case, it doesn't really matter because, as I told you, there's no Iphigenia here to be found. Find yourself some other poor wretch to harass."

He stood aside, gesturing with exaggerated courtesy towards the door. Alix looked desperately around the room, but now none of the men would meet her eyes and she realised that it was futile to stay any longer. With a final glare at the tall Greek who waited so implacably for her to leave, she stalked out and marched on trembling legs down the sunlit street.

Only when she was well out of sight of the

taverna, around a corner, did she stop and lean against the wall. Her whole body was shaking, and tears stung her eyes. Angrily, she dashed them away with her hand and bit her lip hard to prevent more from falling.

What in the name of heaven was it all about? Why had that insufferable Greek taken it upon himself to decide that her search for Iphigenia must be in some way wrong, that it would disturb the old woman's life? Of course, there was the possibility that she had married, that reminders of her past would be unwelcome — but Alix already knew that, and intended to respect it. But the Greek didn't know — couldn't know — why she was here. So how could he make judgements?

Alix shook her head. It was beyond her. But as she stood gazing out over the olive groves towards the glittering blue waters of the bay, she knew one thing with complete certainty.

No Greek chef, however arrogant and however important he considered himself in his local community, was going to stop her in her search. She would find Iphigenia, as she had promised to do. And then she would enjoy the rest of her time on Crete before going back to London to pick up the threads of her own life.

And no man, however arrogant, however commanding, however attractive — damn him — was going to get into her hair, her mind or her heart the way Rick had done.

No way!

It took a little while for Alix to recover herself, but when an old man came creaking down the street, staring curiously at her, she pulled herself together and walked quickly out of the village, past the little church. She had intended going inside to look at it, but the feeling that the hostile Greek was still about, perhaps watching her at this very minute, drove her on past it and down a narrow path leading through the olive groves. Once safely hidden amongst the trees, she sat down on a rock and pulled a bottle of water from her rucksack.

The cool drink restored her a little, but she still felt oddly shaken. The encounter with the Greek had disturbed her more than she would have expected. After all, she was no delicate blossom — for all her petite figure — and had been able to look after herself very well in the cut-and-thrust of London's magazine world.

In fact, that had been one of her problems — that her apparent fragility always seemed to bring out one of two reactions in the men she met. Either they treated her as an empty-headed bimbo, or they tried to take care of her. They didn't exactly tell her not to bother her pretty little head, but the implication was there.

Alix knew, and had proved, that she was intelligent and capable, and she knew too that she needed a man who would not only recognise this, but appreciate and enjoy it. But so far, every time she had found a man who seemed as if he

57

might be the right one, her capabilities seemed to have scared him off. Some men seemed literally afraid of a capable woman — as if they felt their own position were threatened. She had been accused of being hard, ruthless, a feminist and even, once or twice, a second Lady Thatcher — yet, to her mind, all she wanted was to be a woman, without having to apologise for it.

Since Rick had let her down so cruelly, she had begun to despair of ever finding a man who could accept her without feeling threatened by her. And she had told herself that she didn't need one anyway. Who wanted the hassle of a man, when a single life could be so fulfilling, when alone you could go anywhere, do anything, the world your oyster, without having once to consider someone who would inevitably want to be in charge? Who *needed* that?

And she had protected herself by growing what she thought of as an extra skin — a sort of shell, or armour, which she slid into every morning before going out to face the world.

So far, it had worked well. No man had got under this extra skin, though several had tried, deceived as always by her diminutive figure and wide green eyes. And she had felt confident that by now she could deal with whatever male came her way. Until today . . .

Damn him! she thought with sudden viciousness. Why does he have to come muscling into my life, just when I'd got it all so nicely sorted out? All I had to do was come to Crete, spend a

58

week or two enjoying myself and find Iphigenia for Grandfather. In a couple of weeks I'll be back in London, starting a new job. Why does he have to spoil it all?

She sat for several minutes angrily tearing with her fingers at the grass, then laughed at herself for getting all uptight about a man she'd never seen before and would certainly never see again, once she was off this island — for if there was one thing she was certain of, it was that she would never go near the Minos restaurant again, just in case . . .

There I go again, she thought ruefully. Why am I letting him get to me, when I've successfully fended off so many others? What did he have that they didn't — apart from the darkest, most liquid brown eyes she had ever seen, a profile that would have had Narcissus throwing away his mirror, black curls in which a girl could lose all her fingers and a body to rival Stallone's?

She smiled. What else did he need? But she knew it wasn't his physical attributes that had got to her, impressive though they were. It was the sheer power of his personality.

Too powerful for his own good. But didn't power also spell energy, capacity, authority, vigour — all the things she admired most in a man?

Maybe, but it could also spell arrogance. And conceit and domination. All the things she didn't admire at all.

Well, none of it mattered anyway. Whoever he

was, she'd steer clear of him from now on. What was most annoying was that he'd ruined her search — for today, at least. Whatever he thought she was doing here — and she was completely baffled by his insinuations that she'd come to harass Iphigenia — he'd effectively made an end to any co-operation on the part of the village men. And it was clear to her that what she most needed was an interpreter — someone who could speak Greek and explain to the villagers what she wanted. Someone with the tact and sensitivity to tread carefully on what might, it seemed, be thin ice.

He could have been just the person, she thought with irritation. But there was clearly no way he was going to help her. So — who else was there?

She thought again of Gil. He spoke Greek, very well, it appeared. And he was friendly, and alone here. But somehow she wasn't sure she wanted to enlist his help in her search. Pleasant though he was, there'd been something in the way he'd looked at the sketch of Iphigenia on the plane, that she hadn't quite liked. Something that spoke of more than ordinary interest — a kind of curiosity she couldn't quite define . . .

But surely any man would look at that sketch with interest. Iphigenia had been a girl of extraordinarily arresting beauty. And Ian McConnell had drawn her with the hand of love.

Alix got to her feet and began to wander slowly

down the twisting little path through the olive grove, back to Plakias. The sun was hotter now and she was thankful for the shade of her wide-brimmed straw hat. The warm scent of herbs drifted about her head, and out on the bay she could see the white wings of a yacht in full sail. She stopped again, settling herself on a hummock of grass, picking idly at the wild sage as she gazed out across the glittering blue sea.

Her grandfather had sat somewhere near here — perhaps in this very spot — looking out to sea with Iphigenia. He had been watching for the invaders he had come to fight, for the Germans who were taking over the islands. Greeks and Cretans had battled ferociously to save their homeland, and the Australians, the New Zealanders and the British had fought with them, but in the end the might of the attackers had proved too much and the Allies had been forced to evacuate.

The Cretans might have seen this as a betrayal. But instead, they still revered the memories of those who had come to save them and been defeated. There were still plaques of remembrance to be found, there were still old people who remembered with warmth and gratitude — like the old men in the café who must have been here then, who had known the Allied soldiers, had seen them driven away by the hated Germans.

Some of them might even have known her grandfather. They *must* have known Iphigenia.

She felt a fresh spurt of anger against the arrogant Cretan who had spoiled her investigations. And a fresh determination to succeed in her quest, in spite of him.

Alix looked out again at the bay, trying to imagine what it must have been like to sit here, knowing that your life was in danger, that at any moment the enemy might come upon you. There would have been no quarter given, she knew that, no mercy. Her grandfather — and his sweetheart Iphigenia, together with all her family — could have been executed without further ado.

It seemed almost impossible to imagine that such acts could take place in this peaceful spot. And yet . . .

Peaceful though Crete might appear today, it was an island where violence had stalked throughout all its history. Violence between villages; violence between families.

Vendetta . . .

Alix shivered suddenly and scrambled to her feet, walking more quickly this time. It was as if a ghost walked at her shoulder, as if the menace that had threatened her grandfather had returned to haunt her. As if a cloud had shadowed the sun, even though it shone as brightly as ever. But whereas before its heat had been warm and kind, now it was harsh and dangerous.

I must find her, she thought with sudden urgency. I must find Iphigenia. And then perhaps I'll be able to get on with my own life.

The path wound on through the olive grove. Every now and then, through the silvery branches, Alix caught a glimpse of the bay far below. The white sand was brightened with a scatter of blue umbrellas and sunbathers, with a few early swimmers braving the water, still cold as yet. There were none of the crowds that Alix supposed must come later in the year, and the scene was pleasant and peaceful.

Up here, under the olive trees, it was cool, though the sun shone warmly in the small clearings and she guessed that down there on the beach it might be quite hot. She felt no envy for the bathers, however. Alix liked swimming and enjoyed the occasional afternoon on the beach, but her real pleasure was in the countryside, where she could feel at peace, away from the hubbub of crowded streets.

Not that she didn't enjoy London too. She loved the bustle and excitement of working in one of the world's greatest capital cities, with people of all nations jostling together. She enjoyed being able to see the best shows and hear the best concerts, and liked the feeling of being at the centre of things. And she'd loved her job on the magazine. Science had always been her best subject at school, but after taking her physics degree at university she hadn't been quite sure what she wanted to do. Teaching didn't appeal and she didn't want to hide away in a research laboratory. The chance to work on a leading magazine, presenting scientific news and topics to a wide range of readers, from the interested layman to the leading physicist, was one she had leapt at.

When Rick had dropped his bombshell and she'd decided she must get away from London for a while, she'd thought she would have to give up her job as features editor. But to her astonishment, her boss John Kitchener had offered her an even better job instead.

"Have your break," he'd said, looking at her kindly over the top of his glasses. "We don't want this new section to start just yet. By the time you come back, we'll be ready to start the planning. Go off and enjoy yourself for a few months, and forget that idiot who didn't know a good thing when he had it."

Alix had laughed, though at the time she didn't feel at all like laughing, and done as she was told. And when she'd returned to London from New Zealand and gone to the office, she'd been told that they would start planning the new section in three weeks' time — just long enough for this visit to Crete.

She paused, gazing at a huge olive tree. It looked almost as if it had once been a whole cluster of little trees which had huddled together so tightly they had finally become one. Its branches spread wide over the bare ground, and underneath it were the nets that caught the ripe olives as they fell, ready to be gathered up.

Beyond the tree, she could see the walls of a

building. She approached slowly, wondering if she had come to another village, or perhaps to someone's home set high up on the cliffs, and then realised that it was a ruin.

It looked like a ruined monastery. With a beat of excitement, she remembered that her grandfather had been hidden in an old monastery. Could this be the one? She went forward, thinking of him lying here, concealed above the bay while he waited for rescue, tended by the women who came from the village . . . Tended by the beautiful young girl he had fallen in love with . . .

The walls were broken in places, but mostly still standing, and she walked around them touching the mellow stone. This end looked as if it might be a small church, and as she rounded the corner she saw that this was so, and that the church was still complete, its door solid and secure.

She tried the door and it swung open, so silently that she knew before she stepped inside that the church must be still cared for. She stood for a moment letting her eyes get used to the darkness, and then gasped.

Outside, the church was bare and plain, its stucco green with age and flaking away from the walls. Inside, it was a glory.

Alix stared around her at the painted walls, wishing she had brought a torch so that she could see them better. Every inch of wall space was covered with religious pictures, painted in the brilliant blues, reds and golds of stained glass. There was a small screen, glimmering with what must surely be gold leaf, and above it, his arms spreading over the ceiling in blessing, a representation of Christ in Majesty which dominated the tiny building.

On the minute altar stood a single candlestick, holding a candle which had burned down to a stump. Beside the door, Alix found a box of candles and some matches. She lit one and used it to replace the stump, so that the flickering light shed a soft, mellow light on the paintings. There was a bottle of oil and one of wine, or perhaps water, as well — votive offerings, she thought. Clearly, this church was still loved and cared for, and probably used regularly.

Her grandfather had told her about the little churches dotted all over Crete. Some were ornately decorated inside, others no more than bare caves hewn out of the rock. You could stand in a wide valley, he said, and look around at half a dozen little domes and spires, each of them carefully tended, cherished as the heart of the community.

Some of them had provided sanctuary for the soldiers taking cover in the deep countryside. In one, perhaps this very one, attached to the ancient monastery, he had met Iphigenia.

Reluctantly, aware of a deep sense of peace, Alix turned to go. She closed the door softly behind her and walked on around the walls, turning the next corner to find a small wired enclosure with a few chickens scratching about on the earth. It looked as if someone lived here — an old monk, perhaps. But there was no sign of a person, nor any sound.

The building here seemed to be in relatively good repair. Curiously, Alix went closer, and found a door standing open. She peered into the dimness within.

After a moment or two, she could see that the room was clearly lived in. There was a small table, a chair or two, a sideboard with photographs on it. She caught sight of a stove in one corner, and a narrow bed.

Unable to resist it, she went a little closer, wondering who could possibly be living here, in this ruined monastery. A caretaker of some sort, she assumed, and thought of the little church. It had been obvious that someone tended it.

I oughtn't to be here, she thought suddenly, feeling guilty. This is someone's home. But it was the first truly Cretan home she had seen, and she could not resist a quick peep at the photographs before leaving. Photographs of a family — children, held in the arms of stern fathers and proud mothers; old people, their faces a mass of wrinkles. And one of a young girl, dressed for her wedding in a long, sweeping gown of elaborate lace ruffles.

"What the hell are you doing here?"

Alix jumped violently. She turned, her heart hammering against her ribs, and stared at the man who was standing in the doorway, filling it with his bulk, his whole posture one of threat and anger.

It was the Greek from the taverna.

Chapter Four

For a long moment, they stared at each other — the huge Greek filling the doorway with solid menace, and Alix, small and scared — and guilty.

"I — I'm sorry," she stammered at last. "I know I shouldn't be here. I — I was just passing and noticed — I couldn't help seeing the door was open. I just wanted to see if anyone was here, I didn't mean . . ."

Her stammers died away and she gazed up at him, her green eyes wide. He had shifted slightly so that she could see his face, and she wished he hadn't. That look of fury was enough to scare off the devil himself. She looked past him at the bright sunshine, the shadows under the olive trees, and wondered how she could escape.

"You weren't *'just passing'*," he said, speaking slowly and with what seemed to her to be quite unnecessary emphasis. "You *'couldn't help seeing that the door was open'*. You *'just wanted to see if anyone was here'*. Well I can accept all those things. But," and voice suddenly hardened, so that Alix jumped, "you *could* help stopping to look. You *could* help coming in through that door. And you certainly *couldn't* expect someone to step out of one of those photographs you were studying with such interest!" His sarcasm was biting as the fangs of a savage dog. "My God, I wonder what you'd say if someone wandered into your flat in London and poked around *your* private belongings as if they were on display in some kind of tourist shop! Just because people on Crete live differently, just because they're friendly and welcoming and *invite* visitors into their homes, just because they trust their neighbours sufficiently to leave their doors unlocked when they go out of sight for a few minutes — it doesn't mean they can be treated like animals in a zoo, with no rights to human privacy, not even a little courtesy. This isn't one big playground where people like you can saunter in and out of other people's homes as if you owned them." He paused, his eyes glittering with anger, his glance sweeping her so scathingly that Alix felt stripped to the bone. "Nor is it a place where you and your kind can pry into other people's lives simply to further your own squalid little interests. I told you this morning — go back to London. Forget why you came to Crete, and turn your attention to the rest of the gutter, where you can feed off each other and leave the rest of us to get on with our lives."

Alix stared at him. Never in her life had she been spoken to so harshly, so cruelly. She felt as if every shred of breath had been blasted from her body, leaving her empty of the power either to move or to speak. She opened her mouth, but no words formed, and she could only shake her head slowly, and wait for the roaring in her ears to subside and the strength to return.

"Well?" he demanded after a few moments. "Have you nothing to say? No defence?"

Alix found her voice at last.

"I'm sorry," she said tightly. "I know I had no right to come in. I know I shouldn't even have stopped to look. I — I can't explain why I did, I can only apologise. To the owner," she added quickly, determined not to apologise to *him*. "But I don't see why you have to take it quite so seriously. I'm not stealing anything. I'm not prying —"

"You *are* stealing," he stated flatly. "You're stealing a person's privacy. You're stealing their right to call their home their own. And you were most definitely prying."

Alix bit her lip. He was right, she knew he was right — she just hated admitting it to him. She said, "Very well. I've said I'm ready to apologise for that. But as for your other remarks — as for why I came to Crete, that's none of your business. I don't know what you think I'm doing, but whatever idea you've got into your head, it's wrong. You can't possibly know who or what I am or why I'm here. And I certainly don't intend to tell you. And now, if you'd just stand aside so that I can get out of here, I'll be on my way and hopefully we need never see each other again!"

The speech made her feel better. She tilted her head, looking up at him, defiance sparking in her eyes. Her lips were set firmly together, her small chin jutting a little. Her heartbeat was returning to normal, though it would never, she thought, slow down completely while she was in this man's vicinity. His presence was too powerful, his masculinity like an aura surrounding his body. To come within a yard of him would be to enter that aura, to be pulled into its power as a meteorite might be pulled by the gravity of a planet. Or, she thought, extending the metaphor, like a spaceship sucked into a black hole.

Anyone who had ever read modern science fiction knew what happened to such spaceships. They were never seen again.

"Please," she said, so coolly that the word was a demand rather than a request, "let me pass."

The Greek did not move.

"There's room to pass," he said, indicating the narrow space between his body and the doorjamb.

Alix glanced at it. "Room for a stick insect, perhaps," she said. "Not room for me."

"But then," he said, with a disparaging glance at her small, slim figure, "you're not much bigger than a stick insect yourself, are you?"

Alix felt a spurt of anger. How dared he sneer at her body! Small she might be, but everything was in proportion and in the right place, and more than one man had made plain his admiration.

"Let me pass at once!" she said imperiously.

"You know perfectly well I can't get out until you move. And unless you intend holding me prisoner —"

"An enticing idea," he drawled, letting his eyes move more slowly over her body. "Perhaps you're not quite so much of a stick insect as I first thought. More like a luscious little fly, walking straight into a spider's web."

Alix's anger grew, but it was spiced now with a tremor of alarm. Until now, although all too vibrantly aware of the man's potent masculinity, she hadn't seen him as a real physical threat. But how did she know how dangerous he was? And just how lonely was it in these olive groves? She had seen no one else during her walk up to Sellia, nor since she had left the village. And where was the caretaker who lived here?

She began to wish she had never come this way, never found the monastery, never stopped to peep into the little church. And certainly that she had never strayed into this bare little room with its few pieces of furniture and its mementoes.

"Let me out!" she demanded again, her voice quivering a little. "You've no right to keep me here."

"But you have no right to *be* here," he pointed out. "And since you *have* intruded, I'd say you've given up any other rights you might have, wouldn't you agree?"

"No, I wouldn't!" she snapped. "And I think if you knew anything about law —"

"But I do. English and Cretan. Which is more, I suspect, than you do." He smiled at her, his teeth white against the dark shadows of his face. "But it's an interesting point. We must debate it sometime."

"Thanks, but I'd rather not debate anything with you." Alix went a little nearer, cautiously, still afraid of coming within that aura. She wished she had the courage to push him aside. The courage *and* the strength, she thought bitterly, looking at the massive body and mentally railing against the superior physical strength which gave some men the idea that they had the right to use it to intimidate women. "All I want is to be able to get out of here, preferably before the owner comes back."

"So you do admit you're in the wrong?"

"I already have. Now, *please*, let me pass —"

"But I've already told you — you can walk past me any time you please. There's plenty of room." He glanced at the space, still no wider. "I'm sure a slender little thing like you can squeeze through a gap that size. You have eyes like a cat, after all — surely you have other feline attributes."

"Yes, as it happens, I have." Alix lifted her hands. "Claws. And I'm quite ready to use them if you won't let me out." She smiled at the first sign of shock on his face. "You should never tease pussycats, you know, they don't like it."

"I see. So you're ready to use all the old female ploys — if you can't get your way by stamping your feet and yelling, you'll sink to physical force."

"And isn't that just what you're doing?" Alix flared. "You know perfectly well you're keeping me here by using your size and strength. *You* descended to using force right at the start. And I haven't been stamping my feet and yelling —" she realised that her voice was rising steadily and made an effort to bring it down a few decibels "— I've been *asking*, quite politely I think in the circumstances. *You* did all the yelling, when you gave me that speech about privacy and stealing, and told me to go back to the gutter." She stopped for a deep breath, then continued swiftly. "I've admitted I was in the wrong to come in — I've said I'll apologise to the owner. All you're doing now is playing with me, and I might remind you that as well as a right to privacy, human beings also have a right not to be held against their will. It's called abduction in my country. But perhaps that right doesn't apply in Crete?"

He stared at her, his dark brows drawn together. His eyes were unfathomable, like deep brown wells, and his firm lips pressed together as if in deep thought. He seemed to consider for a moment, then shrugged slightly.

"Very well. I promise not to use force to keep you any longer." He moved a few inches to one side. "There. You now have enough room to pass."

Barely enough, Alix thought, but she recognised that this concession was as far as he was likely to go. Antagonise him any further and there was no knowing what he might do. She eyed the gap, knowing that she would still be forced to pass closer to him than she would have liked, then moved forward.

His body emitted warmth, and a musty scent which seemed to come straight from his surroundings — from the olive trees, from the blazing yellow sorrel beneath them, from the very soil of Crete. The aura she had sensed and feared struck her almost like a wall, then melted and merged around her, its power soaking into her skin to vibrate through flesh and muscle right to her very bones. She felt his masculinity like a shock, felt her own deeply primitive female response and knew that this was what she had feared, what she had recognised, from the first moment she had seen him on the plane, as the secret source of his power over her. Over any woman, she thought, staring up as if mesmerised into the dark face. Over *every* woman . . .

He was close, so close that there could be no more than a breath between their bodies. She could feel the prickle of her skin, as if her nerves were reaching out to him, wanting to be touched, wanting to expose their exquisite sensitivity to his, as if by being so close were in itself a caress.

She had stopped, there in the doorway, stopped as if her body refused to move another step. As if the sensuality of her nature, a sensuality that had never before been permitted full rein, had recognised a kindred spirit, a mate. As if thought and sophistication and all that went to make up a modern woman were nothing beside this deep, primeval urge to make contact with its own affinity.

This is ridiculous, she thought wildly. I've got to move, got to get a distance between me and this man. But even as the thought formulated, she saw the sudden darkening of his eyes, eyes already a deep, velvet brown, to full black with no more than a rim of glittering bronze, and she knew that he had felt the impact as well.

"We-e-ell," he murmured huskily, and with a slow, almost lazy movement, took her in his arms and laid his mouth upon hers.

Alix trembled. The aura was now all about her, wrapping her in a drifting cloud of sensual rapport that undermined all her senses and drove out every thought, leaving her conscious only of need, a leaping flame of desire that she knew was entirely mutual and brought their bodies almost clashing together with an urgency she had never experienced, never imagined, and had neither power nor wish to resist.

His arms enfolded her, her slender body almost lost in his muscular strength. But there was strength too in her own delicately-shaped hands, in the fingers that splayed themselves across his back, stroking the shoulder blades she could feel beneath the thin shirt. There was strength in the arms she clasped about him and in the kiss she returned to him, her tongue rivalling his as they explored each other's mouths; and there was strength in her body as she strained closer to him, feeling each hard muscle against her softness, feeling her heart jolt against her ribs as she recognised the depth of his arousal.

Neither heard the sudden flurry of the hens scratching about the earth a few yards away. But neither could fail to hear, nor to be startled by, the sudden strident crow of the cockerel almost at their feet. Taken totally by surprise, not even perceiving at first what the sound was, Alix jumped away from the Greek's arms. For a few seconds they stood, both trembling, staring at each other. And then Alix moved again, aware still of the danger and instinctively seeking the safety of distance.

Already, she was beginning to feel the shock of reaction, the burn of shame and anger, the need to blame him for what had just happened.

"How dare you . . ." she began, her voice shaking, but before she could say more another sound made her turn and she realised that they were no longer alone.

An old woman had come into the clearing. She was, like so many of the old women Alix had already seen on Crete, dressed in the rusty black skirt and blouse, with a shawl about her shoulders, that was the traditional dress of the Cretan peasant. She was less bent than many of the others, but her face was brown from long exposure to the sun, and deeply wrinkled. She could have been anything from seventy to ninety years old. She looked from the Greek to Alix and her eyes twinkled.

"Lukas!" she said, her face crackling with pleasure into a network of even more wrinkles. She went on in Greek, evidently asking him about Alix, and Alix, recovering a little, felt her own mouth twitch as she watched him colour and stumble over his answer. Whatever he said, it seemed to please the old woman, however, and she turned to Alix with a broad smile and held out both hands as if in welcome.

Alix gave the man beside her a quick glance of query, but there was nothing she could do but take the hands held out to her and nod at the flood of words which passed straight over her head. Obviously he hasn't told her I was trespassing in her house! she thought, with some relief at having escaped the embarrassment of having to apologise. But what in the name of goodness *has* he told her?

Whatever it was, the old woman was evidently pleased about it. Probably it was nothing more than the fact that Alix was an English tourist and had eaten at the taverna last night, she thought, remembering stories of the hospitality shown by the islanders. Two of her mother's friends had been here a year ago, walking in the hills, and had told her how they had been accosted by old men in vineyards and given wine, how they had been almost dragged bodily into cottages and

79

plied with dishes of pumpkin seeds, coffee and glasses of brandy — even, on one occasion, a meal they strongly suspected had been intended for the family supper but dared not refuse for fear of giving offence. This old woman was showing no more than the same warm pleasure at meeting a visitor to her island, and as she drew Alix nearer to the door of her tumbledown home in the ruined monastery, it became clear that she too was determined to send the guest on her way refreshed.

"Oh — no." The old woman hobbled through the door, leaving them outside, and Alix gave her companion a quick glance of entreaty. "Please — I can't take anything from her. She has so little . . ."

"However little one has, there is always some to share," the man said. "At least, that's the philosophy of my people. It's different in London, I know, where everyone is out to grab everything possible. You will cause her much offence if you refuse."

"But why should she *want* to give me anything? Why does she seem so pleased to see me? What did you tell her?"

"Oh, nothing much," he said blandly. "Just that you were my fiancée, and —"

"That I'm your *what?*"

"You heard." He was smiling, clearly enjoying her reaction. "Listen, what else could I say? She saw us kissing — and she's seen and known enough kisses to know it wasn't just a casual brush of the lips. She'd be shocked if she thought we'd behave like that before being properly betrothed. You wouldn't have me shock an old lady, would you — and her my own grandmother!"

"Your *grandmother?* But —"

"And why should she not be?" he enquired. "We all have a couple somewhere at the back of a cupboard."

Alix sighed with exasperation. "I'm not saying she shouldn't be your grandmother," she hissed. "I just don't see why you think you have the right to tell such lies about me. It's nothing to do with her blushes — it's just to save your own reputation. I refuse to be involved."

"But you *are* involved," he pointed out. "You nodded and smiled at everything she said just now — all about our engagement and wedding —"

"*Wedding?* Now listen —"

"It's all right," he said, grinning, "it won't go that far. Heaven forbid! The last thing I want to do is get myself tied up to a little wildcat like you. Not that it wouldn't have its compensations," he added thoughtfully, and Alix felt the scarlet colour run up into her face. "No, you need have no fear, I have no intention of letting our engagement take us to the altar. In fact, you can break it off as soon as you like —"

"How about now?" she interrupted, but he went on as if she hadn't even spoken.

"— so long as you just let it run long enough to

81

leave my grandmother with her peace of mind. Knowing her grandson is a man of honour, you understand."

"Conned into a false impression, you mean," Alix muttered, but as the old woman came out again, staggering under the weight of a tray laden with bowls and glasses, she knew that it would be impossible for her to refute his lies. She could not be the cause of changing the look of pleasure and pride on the wrinkled face to one of distress and dismay.

"All right, I'll go along with it now," she whispered angrily, "but this is going to be the shortest-lived engagement on record. And I might as well warn you that I'm a rotten liar. I'll probably give the whole game away the minute I open my mouth."

"A rotten liar?" he uttered, his eyes dancing. "Oh come, you can't expect me to believe that — not in your line of business. Anyway, you've no need to worry, I've told her you're terribly shy and hardly likely to say a word." And before she could answer him, her mouth gaping in astonishment, he planted a swift kiss on her cheek and went forward to help his grandmother.

Her line of business? What on earth did he mean? Alix gave her head a baffled shake and then dragged out a smile for the old woman as the erring grandson took the heavy tray and laid it on a small table covered with green oil-cloth, set under one of the spreading olive trees. And then, another thought striking her, she hastily crossed the little yard to his side and hissed into his ear, "I don't even know your name."

"There, you see," he murmured back, "you're getting the idea already. Didn't you hear my grandmother call me by it a few minutes ago? It's Lukas — Lukas Stavroulakis. Perhaps I'd better know yours too — I already know your surname, of course."

"I'm amazed you don't know the entire details of my birth certificate, since you seem to think you know so much else about me," she retorted scathingly, but added with some reluctance, "It's Alix. With an 'i'."

"With two eyes," he said, depositing a light kiss on each of them, "and very pretty ones too, especially when they spark fire as they did a few moments ago."

Alix cast an agonised glance over her shoulder. The old woman was watching them, smiling and nodding, and she smiled weakly back, feeling guilt wash over her. However had she come to be acting out this farce, pretending an engagement to a man she didn't even know? And deceiving an old woman into the bargain. Alix had always hated deception of any kind, finding it difficult to tell even the smallest and whitest of lies — and now she was swept up into this ludicrous pretence which, even if it lasted for no more than an afternoon, would make her feel remorseful for months.

Well, it was her own fault for prying where she had no right. She glanced at Lukas as he came out of the hovel, carrying a couple of old metal chairs to set by the table. If this was meant as a punishment, it was certainly effective. He couldn't have found a better one if he really had known her well.

The little feast was now ready and they all sat down round the table. Alix looked at the plates and bowls, knowing that she must eat but certain that every bite would turn to ashes in her mouth. She accepted a glass of wine and lifted it, stretching her mouth into a feeble smile that would probably be construed as maidenly shyness, as Lukas's grandmother made a small speech that was presumably a toast to the happy couple.

Happy couple! she thought wildly as Lukas clinked his glass against hers. Cats and dogs would have nothing on us, if we ever got married! But fortunately that was the last thing that was likely to happen. She might have been manipulated into this farce of an engagement, but in one thing she was heartily in agreement with Lukas — there would definitely be no wedding.

The two Greeks were now conversing rapidly, with much nodding and smiling, much waving of hands. Organising the hymns and seating arrangements, no doubt, Alix thought sourly, keeping a sickly smile pinned to her face. She wondered who was supposed to pay for weddings in Crete, and thought of her mother's face if she were to get the bill. And where would they live — in a ruined monastery? Or possibly over the taverna. Perhaps Lukas would expect her to help with the washing-up.

The old grandmother offered her a bowl of salted almonds and she took one and murmured *'Efharisto'*. It was quite a party, she thought, surprised that there should have been such elegant snacks to hand in the simple little home. As well as the nuts there was a bowl of pumpkin seeds, another of some kind of savoury potato snack, and a plate of *baclava*. The wine, she realised, taking a sip, was very good.

The old woman was regarding her intently. Her brown eyes were as dark as Lukas's, set in a web of criss-crossing wrinkles, but they were kind and Alix felt another stab of shame at the deception she and Lukas were practicing. Would it have mattered so very much, she wondered, if he had been found kissing a girl in his grandmother's doorway, and had to confess she was a virtual stranger?

Well, she had to concede that perhaps the situation could have been quite seriously misconstrued — it had been an extremely passionate, not to say forceful, kiss — even now the memory of it was enough to bring the colour flooding again into her cheeks — and without the commitment of an engagement to go with it, an old Cretan woman, steeped in her island's traditions, might well have been shocked.

So wasn't that *his* problem? He could always have moved out of her way, given her more room to pass. But then, if she hadn't been there in the first place . . .

Alix sighed and gave up. It was useless to think what might, what *ought,* to have happened. It was done now, and here she was, sitting at a table under an olive tree amongst the ruins of an old monastery, looking out over the blue waters of Plakias Bay and toasting her future with two strangers who were chattering away together in a language she couldn't understand. It wasn't just bizarre, it was surreal, she thought, and there was nothing to be done but simply go along with it until she and Lukas could decently go on their way.

Then the 'engagement' could be broken off, before they even got as far as Plakias. And the next time Lukas visited his grandmother, he could go through the farce alone — the farce of nursing a broken heart, pulling his life back together again after being jilted almost at the altar. A procedure with which Alix was all too familiar, but which in her case had not been at all farcical. She wondered if Lukas had thought of that.

Well, that *was* his problem. She wouldn't be concerned in it at all. At the thought, she felt her spirits lift and she gave her companions a cheerful smile and lifted her glass again.

"Hey, that's better," Lukas said, giving her knee a pat. "You were beginning to look far too solemn for an engagement party. Poor grandmother was beginning to think she might have upset you."

"*She* thought she'd upset me!" Alix exclaimed, but kept her voice low. She looked across the table and smiled at the old woman, then took a deep breath and tried her few words of Greek. *"Ti kanete?"*

The old face stared back uncomprehendingly, and Lukas smothered a laugh. "What's that supposed to mean?"

" 'How are you'," Alix said, feeling both annoyed and embarrassed. "I'm sure it's right. I learned it specially."

"It must be your accent, then," he said, but at that moment the old woman reached across the table and laid her wrinkled hand on Alix's. Her smile was kind, and her voice soft, but it was her words which startled Alix most, for she spoke in English — halting, heavily accented English, but English nevertheless.

"You are . . . welcome . . . here," she said slowly, dragging each word out from some long disused memory, like someone searching through an old cupboard for a set of rusty tools. "Is good to . . . to see Lukas . . ." she fumbled for the word, "happy. Good." She nodded, her face creasing with smiles.

Alix stared at her.

"You speak English!" Nothing like stating the obvious, she thought.

The old woman laughed and waved a deprecating hand. "Little only. Is long time . . ."

"She learned it when she was young," Lukas said briefly. "A lot of people did."

When she was young . . . Alix gazed at her. Just

how old was she? It was so difficult to tell — and the fact that Lukas was her grandson didn't help at all. She might have grandchildren from their babyhood right up to their forties.

But she was surely old enough to remember the war.

Alix's heart jumped suddenly. *Might she not also remember Iphigenia?*

They could have been contemporaries — friends, she thought with a beat of excitement. And she spoke English. *She* would be able to help . . .

Alix turned her head, looking for her rucksack which she had dropped outside the door of the hovel when she first went in. Spurred on by her excitement, she half rose to her feet — but found herself firmly pushed back into her seat by Lukas's hand, planted solidly on her shoulder.

"No," he said, quietly enough but so forcefully that she could not doubt that he understood her intention. Startled and angry, she turned on him, but the look on his face as he flicked his eyes towards his grandmother prevented her from saying what she wanted to say. Instead, she bit her lip and watched as he turned to the old woman and spoke quickly. The old face creased again in laughter and she nodded and creaked to her feet, then hobbled back into the cottage.

"What was all that about?" Alix hissed. "What did you say to her?"

"Only that we ought to have some coffee before we start to walk down to Plakias. She wouldn't want any accidents to happen because of the quality of her wine!" He smiled tenderly at her, but his tone was anything but loving. "And I know just what was going through your mind then, dear Alix. Don't even think of it."

"Think of what?" she prevaricated, and he snorted.

"You know perfectly well what. Don't think of getting out that drawing and asking her about your friend — what was her name?"

"Iphigenia," Alix muttered sulkily, certain that he had not forgotten.

"Yes. Well, as I said, don't mention her. Don't let the thought even cross your mind. I've already told you — she's not in this area any more, and if you start looking for her you'll simply stir up trouble. And you wouldn't want to do that, would you?"

"Wouldn't I just — if it was for you," she said feelingly, and he smiled.

"I dare say. But you're not going to, are you? Because I warn you, the trouble would be for you, and you alone." He paused for a moment, then added, "Trouble there would certainly be for you — I'd see to that — but the real trouble would be for Iphigenia — if you were to find her. An old woman not unlike my grandmother, who deserves a little peace at the end of her life, wouldn't you say?"

He rose to his feet to go and help his grandmother, lithe and graceful as a tiger. And about twice as dangerous, she thought, staring up at him. That hadn't been a warning he'd uttered, with that affectionate smile on his face the whole time. It had been a threat.

Why? What had happened to her grand-father's sweetheart, to bring such danger to her if she were connected with him, after all these years? Why had she left the area, and where had she gone? And why was this man so concerned to keep her secret?

Whatever the answers, Alix knew that she could not leave Crete without finding them. And there was nothing this arrogant Greek, with his sweeping assumptions and manipulative ways, could do to stop her.

All the same, she could have done without his particular brand of savage masculinity, and even more without her own disconcerting — almost frightening — response to it. And she made up her mind that once they were out of this totally unnecessary and stupid situation, she would steer well clear of him. Wouldn't let herself get within six feet of him.

There was no way she was going to risk coming within range of that strange, compelling and positively *dangerous* aura again.

Chapter Five

The impromptu engagement party at the old monastery was over at last, and Alix and Lukas set off down the path which wound down the cliffs towards the bay. This was something she could well have done without, Alix thought as she followed the Greek's broad figure through the olive groves. Afternoon strolls in the woods with a man who had managed to frighten her, kiss her — with devastating effect — and manipulate her into a mock engagement, all within the space of half an hour, were in no way on her agenda. But there was little she could do about it, in the face of his grandmother's obvious delight and the good wishes uttered in her rusty English. It would have looked peculiar in the extreme if she and Lukas had gone their separate ways.

All the same, Alix had no intention of letting the situation drag on a second longer than it had to. And she told him so, in no uncertain terms, as soon as she judged they were safely out of his grandmother's earshot.

"I don't like lying to anyone, least of all an old lady who's never done me the slightest harm," she finished, talking to his back as he marched ahead of her. "I felt terrible, sitting there drinking her wine and eating her food and *pretending*. As for you — surely it would be far worse if she found you were a liar than if she knew you were simply the sort of man who . . . who . . ." Her voice trailed away as she sought for the words to describe the sort of man he was.

"Who assaults young ladies in lonely places?" he supplied helpfully, not turning his head. "You'd rather be raped than lied to, is that it? Not that you were in any danger," he added, without noticeable haste, "but I can see that you would have had no scruples about making it look like that. You think my grandmother would have preferred that to a few little white lies?"

"But they're not white lies!" Alix said explosively. "They're *lies* — out and out lies, that I'd rather not be involved in. Especially since it seems that we're telling them more to save your skin than your grandmother's sensibilities. Couldn't you have said something else? Couldn't you have just told her that — oh, that we'd met on holiday and were just having a little fling, or something? Did it have to be an *engagement?*"

"D'you know, that just never occurred to me," he said blandly, and she could tell from his voice that he was smiling. "Perhaps I didn't see you as the sort of girl who would indulge in 'flings'. But then I could have been wrong about that."

He stopped, so suddenly that Alix walked straight into his back. But no, it wasn't his back. In the same instant he'd turned, and she found

92

herself pressed hard against his chest, with his powerful arms wrapped tightly around her.

"Let me *go!*" she stormed, banging her fists uselessly against his shoulders. "How dare you! Let me go at once!"

But even as she shouted at him, she knew that her words were carrying less and less conviction. That damned aura was getting to her again. The almost tangible essence of him, wafting around her, engulfing her in a wave of sexuality. She gazed up at him, seeing from the darkening of his eyes and the sudden tension in his face that he felt it too. Another moment and he'd be kissing her again, she thought, lowering her eyes hastily, and that she just could not bear.

"Please," she said, and her voice trembled in an agony of dismay, anger and wholly unwelcome desire, "let me go."

Lukas hesitated for a moment and she braced herself for his kiss. Then, to her astonishment, he released her, so abruptly that she almost staggered. His hand shot out involuntarily to catch her and for a few seconds there was a throb of danger that he might pull her back into his arms. Then his hand fell away and Alix stepped back, aware of both relief and, from her treacherous body, regret.

"You've got to stop this," she said, her voice still shaking. "I can't handle it. Look, I didn't come to Crete for a holiday romance, nor a life-long commitment. As far as I'm concerned, both are irrelevant. I came for a purpose —"

His face hardened. "I know that. I know your purpose."

Alix stared at him, baffled. What did he mean? How *could* he know? Was an event such as a young soldier's love for a Cretan girl — a *betrothed* Cretan girl, she reminded herself — so important that it could still be reverberating about the island half a century later? Did they really take things as seriously as that?

Vendetta . . . The word echoed menacingly in her mind. Her grandfather had told her stories — stories of families feuding for generations, of battles to the death up in the mountains. And what about *Zorba the Greek*? She had seen the film years ago and only half remembered it, but the fight scene, with knives flashing in the cruel sunlight, had stuck in her memory.

Had Iphigenia been driven out of the village by the scandal of her romance? And were the consequences still creating family quarrels on a scale that Alix, with her British upbringing, couldn't hope to understand?

There was, surely, no other way that Lukas could know why she was here, nor any other reason for his hostility.

"I don't understand," she said wearily. "Why are you so against me? If only you would explain —"

"Are *you* willing to explain to *me?*"

Alix hesitated. A few hours ago, she would have said yes, unhesitatingly, especially as he not only spoke English as well as she did herself but also seemed to know and have the respect of everyone in the area. *And* must have grown up here too, since his grandmother lived in the old monastery. But since he'd made his feelings on the subject so clear, it was impossible for her to tell him about her grandfather, living old and crippled on the other side of the world, thinking and wondering about his lost love, needing to know that she fared well. Who knew but what the tendrils of these large, involved Cretan families might reach as far as New Zealand — that even now one of Iphigenia's relatives might decide to avenge her honour . . .

Alix shook herself. This was getting ridiculous! Such things didn't happen, not in the nineteen-nineties. But she remembered the village of Sellia, its ancient houses, the people who seemed to be living a way of life that had been the same for a thousand years. The donkeys tethered at the roadside, the old women taking sheep and goats to the pasture. Nothing had altered there for centuries. Why should this one thing have changed?

"You see," Lukas said triumphantly when she remained silent, "you're not prepared to be honest with me. Yet you object to a little bit of a charade to make an old woman feel better about her own family."

"I object to being manipulated into it," she flashed. "You'd no right —"

"I thought," he said silkily, "that we'd already established that it was *you* who had no right — to be where you were, doing what you were doing. But do feel free to correct me if I'm wrong about that too."

Alix turned away, exasperated. There was no way of winning an argument with this man. He was just too slick with words. And it wasn't fair, considering that it was *her* language they were speaking!

"How did you get to be so good at English?" she asked, abandoning the subject of their 'engagement' for the moment. "I suppose you've worked in London."

"You know perfectly well I have," he returned, and once again she remembered the Greek restaurant, the Minos. In the heat of the past hour or two she had forgotten her confusion over whether or not he was the proprietor who had welcomed her in on so many occasions — and who had been there on that last, disastrous night. Now his words confirmed it. "You've spoken to me often enough. Not that I expect you to remember — I was just a servant as far as you were concerned, you and your glamorous job."

Alix gaped at him. Glamorous job? But she supposed that anyone working on a magazine seemed glamorous — she'd had trouble enough explaining to some of her more sceptical friends that science magazines didn't have quite the same cachet as the women's glossies like *Vogue* or *Hello*. Still, she did get to take some of the writers out to lunch occasionally, and a very

boring lot they were too, some of them —
pedantic, fussy about their food, and often with
egos bigger than those of the average film star.

Well, that answered one question — where she
had seen him before. But why was he working in
a Cretan taverna?

"The Minos?" she asked. "Is that where I've
seen you?" And then, defensively in answer to
his contemptuous nod, "I wasn't really sure. I
have an awful memory for faces and I just
couldn't make up my mind whether you were
the man I'd seen in the restaurant. Seeing you in
a different environment, in different clothes . . ."
She floundered to a halt, annoyed by the scepti-
cism of his gaze, and abandoned her attempt to
convince him. She didn't need any more arguments.

"Have you given up the Minos?" she asked. "I
haven't been there for a while — I didn't realise
you'd left it. Did you decide to come back to
Crete?"

"Come back?" he repeated. "Left? But I never
left — either the Minos, or Crete. Ah — I see
what you mean. The taverns. No, I haven't given
up the Minos. I'm here for a week or two only, as
a holiday, but I like to help out while I'm here.
The taverna belongs to my uncle, you see, and
he deserves a night off now and then. That's why
I was working in the kitchen last night."

"I see." She frowned. "But what did you mean
when you said you'd never left? I thought the
restaurant in London was yours."

"So it is. My father's, anyway." He watched her thoughtfully for a moment, then grinned. "All right, pussycat, I won't tease you any more — I haven't forgotten those claws! I've always lived in London. I was born there — grew up there, except for when I was away at school. But my father never forgot his homeland, and he made sure that I always spent a large part of my holidays on Crete, to become a part of my own family here and to learn my own language. So now I have a foot in both camps. I understand and feel a part of both cultures."

"Equally?" she asked curiously. "No more one than the other?" She thought of the almost tribal culture that still pervaded this island, contrasted with the looser family life in England.

Lukas smiled slowly and she was once more aware of the danger that lurked in those dark brown eyes, of the passion that could so easily be aroused in both him and herself. Involuntarily, she took a step back and saw amusement tug at the corners of his mouth. She bit her own lip in annoyance.

"Almost equally, I think," he mused, answering her question. "It depends where I am. When in London, I think I am almost wholly British, with just enough Greek in me to give me the touch I need in my restaurant. But in Crete —" his dark eyes flashed and she shivered "— I would say that I am almost wholly Cretan."

"With just enough British in you to keep you civilized?" she said lightly, and he raised his brows, looking suddenly angry.

"Are you saying that my people are *uncivilised*? Barbarians? Was it the hospitality of an ignorant savage that you received at my grandmother's home just now? Or in the taverna at Sellia this morning?"

Alix bit her lip and cursed herself. "Of course not. I'm sorry. I was thinking of something else."

"Our little encounter in the doorway, perhaps," he suggested, the smoothness returning to his voice. "But I would have said that that was mutual — and wholly delightful. Or perhaps you don't agree there, either." He moved a little closer. "Perhaps we should repeat the experiment, just to be certain that we're describing it with accuracy."

Alix jumped back as if she had been stung. "No! Don't touch me. Don't you dare. I told you, I didn't come here for —"

"A holiday romance," he said, as if repeating a lesson, "nor a lifelong commitment. Yes, you told me. Well, I wasn't looking for such things either. It simply seemed the best way out of an awkward situation."

"Awkward for *you*," she reminded him. "What your grandmother, or anyone else for that matter, thinks of *me* doesn't really come into it. But my own conscience and self-respect do, and I've told you, I don't enjoy lying, especially to old ladies who don't deserve to be treated in such a way. So to get back to what I was saying to start with, you'd better think of some way of ending our so-called engagement as quickly as possible. I don't want to be mixed up in any more play-acting."

"Agreed," he said amiably. "So what do you suggest?"

"What do *I* suggest? It's not for me to suggest anything! You got us — yourself — into this mess. You get out of it." She lifted her chin and met his eyes, her own sparking with challenge. "In fact, I don't really see why I should bother myself any more about it. The whole crazy situation's your doing. You can't force me to go along with it. I shall simply have no more to do with it — or with you. You can tell your grandmother what you like."

There was a long silence. Lukas stared at her, and she quaked at the darkening of his narrowed eyes. His brows were drawn together in a bar of black and the muscles of his face were taut and angry. Almost reflectively, he lifted one hand and stroked his chin; she sensed the violence simmering beneath the surface of his control and felt a panic-stricken urge to turn and run. But she would not let him see that he frightened her. Like a wild animal, if he sensed her fear he might be antagonised still further and lose that precarious control.

"And it doesn't bother you that she'll be hurt, upset, disappointed?" he enquired. "You can live with that?"

It did bother Alix, and she knew that living with it would be uncomfortable. But short of marrying this man and spending the rest of her life with him — a thought too terrifying to contemplate — she couldn't see any way around it. And the old lady would be even more hurt, upset and disappointed if the engagement were permitted to continue, only to be broken at a later stage.

"She's your grandmother," she said tightly. "Not mine."

He nodded his head slowly, as if the response were no more than he had expected. For a moment or two, he seemed to be lost in thought, staring at the rough stony track with its scatter of fallen olives. Then he lifted his head and looked into her eyes.

"Very well. I'll make a bargain with you. I want our apparent engagement to continue for the time being. It would be too much of a shock to my grandmother to have it announced to her and then broken off within the space of a few hours. For her sake, I ask you to keep up the pretence for the next two weeks, while you're here on Crete. Then, when we go back to London, we can part without any strings and need never see each other again. I'll 'break off' the engagement myself, when the time seems right."

"The next *two weeks?*" It seemed a lifetime. "But —"

"In return," he continued as if she had not spoken, "I'll help you look for Iphigenia. Yes, I know I refused, but I had my reasons — good ones — and I have my reasons now for changing my mind. But I think I know where she may be found, if she's still alive, and if she is, and if she agrees, I'll take you to her." He looked into her eyes again and she saw the determination there. "But there's one proviso — that you do nothing, say nothing to her that might cause further trouble. Do you understand?"

"I didn't come here to cause trouble at all —" she began, and he shook his head impatiently.

"Perhaps not, in your terms, but look what's already happened." And before she could make the indignant retort that rose to her lips, he swept on. "Well? Do I have your agreement? My help in finding Iphigenia, in return for your co-operation in keeping my grandmother happy? Is it a bargain?"

Alix gazed at him. He had her in a corner. Without the help of someone who both spoke Greek and understood the local people, she had little chance of tracking down her grandfather's sweetheart. But without her co-operation in his charade, Lukas would not give her that help.

"All right," she said and her voice sounded bleak as the implications of her acquiescence began slowly to sink in, "it's a bargain."

Back in her apartment, safe at last from that magnetic personality, Alix sank down on her bed and contemplated the events of the day.

Well, you really have hit Crete, haven't you! she thought wryly. Less than a day on the island

102

and you've stirred up some sort of ancient controversy, got yourself engaged to a man who's obviously a member of one of the leading families, as well as being a successful London restaurateur, and told heaven knows how many lies to an innocent old woman who's bound to get hurt by them eventually — whether it's today or in six months' time. Or maybe he intends us to stretch our engagement out until she's dead . . .

Well, that was most certainly *his* problem. Alix had agreed to go along with his plan, mainly because there didn't seem to be any other course. And she had to acknowledge that his help would be invaluable. But she didn't intend to get involved any more than was absolutely necessary with his grandmother. The thought of telling even more lies — either through Lukas or through the old woman's own tentative command of English — was one she refused to countenance. And with any luck, they would find Iphigenia quickly — before the end of the week, perhaps. Then Alix could cut her stay short and take the first available plane back to London.

But that wasn't her most immediate concern. More pressing than that was the anxious knowledge that she had committed herself to spending what might be a considerable amount of time with the forceful Greek. If he were to help her find Iphigenia, she would have to talk to him, tell him about her grandfather and that long-ago romance. They would have to go to find the old woman, wherever she was now living, and that meant spending hours, perhaps whole days together, cramped close beside each other in a bus or car. Within range of that dangerous personal space, that aura that seemed to shimmer about him like a cloud, that sense of physical attraction and danger to which her own body — damn it! — responded like wildfire in a tinder-dry forest . . .

Alix shook herself impatiently. What in the world's the matter with you? she asked herself. Anyone would think you were a naive teenager, out in the world for the first time. Surely you've met enough men who think they're God's gift to womankind, to be able to cope with this one. He's no different from the rest — good-looking enough, *rich* enough, to think he's entitled to fumble any girl who happens to stand a little too close. You've never had any problem fending off such types in the past.

No, she thought, but I haven't felt the same response to them either. And I don't understand why I should now.

Simple, the inner voice continued. You've not long been jilted practically at the altar — a traumatic experience for anyone, even if you've since realised that Rick really wasn't the right man for you. Now your emotions are reeling about all over the place. You want to hit out at the first presentable male who comes your way, but you're also frustrated and upset over the way Rick broke things off. You're an adult woman, for goodness' sake, her inner mentor went on as if delivering a lecture. You *want* to be loved. You want *sex*. It's purely biological, really, and all you have to do is realise it and resist him.

Oh, really? Alix thought sardonically, and then almost laughed at herself. What was she doing, lying here on her bed having an argument with herself? Wasn't arguing with Lukas enough for her? Or maybe she needed the practice!

With a swift movement, she swung her legs to the floor and stood up. She stripped off her clothes and walked into the shower room. The water was hot, for the sun had been beating all day on the solar panels on the roof, and she luxuriated under its warm spray, rubbing shampoo into her hair and shower gel over her body as if by so doing she could rid herself of every vestige of Lukas . . .

And suddenly she was crying, her tears mingling with the spray of the shower, her body racked with sobs, all the grief and misery and humiliation of the past few months welling up in her at last, refusing to be suppressed, refusing to go unacknowledged any more.

Oh Rick, Rick, she thought, I hate you for what you've done to me. I hate you, d'you hear me? *Hate* you!

But it wasn't Rick's face she saw in her mind as she stood under the streaming water, shaking. Instead, she saw the dark face and smouldering brown eyes of a tall Greek, as much at home in a city suit in London as wearing a chef's apron, or jeans and a white shirt, here on his native island.

A man who could, she knew without doubt, deal her more pain with one sardonic lift of his eyebrow than Rick had ever done.

What have I got myself into? she asked herself with a surge of terror. And how in the world do I get myself out of it?

The storm of weeping over at last, Alix pulled herself together and stepped out of the shower. Because she had simply let the tears flow, not rubbing or wiping her eyes, they looked less red and swollen than she had feared. She soaked some cotton wool pads in icy water and lay on her bed, pressing them against her face, and then got up and began to dress.

The evening was still warm and she slipped on a *broderie anglaise* blouse with a low, scooped neck, and her multi-coloured skirt. To give herself courage, she picked out the long, brightly coloured earrings and a wooden necklace she had bought in New Zealand, and pushed her feet into thin sandals which matched the main colours in her skirt. Whatever surprises Lukas Stavroulakis might have in store for her this evening, she was ready to face them.

She was sorely tempted to go to a different taverna. But she knew that Lukas would be expecting her, looking out for her, and she needed his help too much to go back on the bargain they had struck. And she also wanted to see Gil again. The Englishman had been friendly enough, even if he wasn't really her type, and heaven knew she needed a friend here on Crete. Anyway, she thought with grim humour, it would be extremely pleasant to have dinner with someone who wasn't her type, and therefore presented no threat to her composure!

The idea made her catch her breath. Was she saying that Lukas *was* her type? Definitely not, she thought, ignoring the quiver of excitement in her wayward body. He's just over-sexed. Too male to be able to forget it, and he gives off something — some kind of scent, perhaps — that probably affects every woman unfortunate enough to come within range of it. It doesn't mean a thing, except that it's wise to keep your distance, since he's obviously quite unscrupulous about taking advantage of it.

And how was she to keep her distance, cooped up with him in a car while they scoured Crete for a woman who might have died long ago?

It occurred to her that he might just be using Iphigenia as an excuse to get Alix alone with him. Wasn't she being foolish — not to say downright crazy — to go along with him?

By the time she reached the bridge, Alix had made up her mind to tell him that the bargain was off. She'd find Iphigenia by herself, thank you very much, or she'd ask Gil to help her. Lukas would bring nothing but trouble, and she was best keeping right out of his way. And if it got him into trouble with his grandmother, well, that was his problem.

She leaned over the low parapet, remembering

how the old lady had held her hands, nodding, smiling and welcoming her in voluble Greek, hobbling into her cottage in the monastery ruins, staggering out again with a tray laden with wine and nuts and crisps. Obviously thrilled and delighted to be entertaining her grandson's fiancée.

Clearly, he was the apple of her eye. And when she learned that he was not, after all, to marry the English girl who had sat at her table, eating her food and drinking her wine, she was going to be very disappointed.

It's not my problem! Alix thought again, trying frantically to banish her picture of the old eyes filling with tears, the wrinkled mouth trembling. It's *not!*

"You're looking very pensive."

Alix jumped and turned quickly, smiling up into Gil's blue eyes. "I was trying to spot the toads. You can hear them croaking quite loudly, but they're difficult to see."

"Perhaps they only come out when it's dark." He leaned against the bridge, looking down at her. "And what have you been doing today? Sunning yourself on the beach?"

Alix shook her head. "I went for a walk up through the olive groves, to Sellia." She waved her hand towards the village, high up on the side of the mountain, and wondered whether to tell him more. Then she needn't be dependent on Lukas, and she could dispense with the charade of their engagement. It was a shame about the old lady, but she was going to be disappointed sooner or later. Where was the sense in prolonging the agony?

She opened her mouth, but before she could speak Lukas himself came out of the taverna, crossing the open patio with all its occupied tables, and holding out his arms in welcome. His face darkened as he glanced from Gil to Alix and then, before she could move, he swept her into his arms and kissed her soundly.

"Alix, my darling! I thought you'd never come. Everyone's waiting for you, and here you are lingering on the bridge." Was she imagining it, or had he developed a slight Greek accent since this afternoon? "Come in, come in, my uncle and aunt have been making preparations ever since I came home to tell them the news." His strong fingers clasped firmly about her wrist, he began to draw her off the bridge, towards the door of the taverna.

Alix had no choice but to go with him. She flung a look at the little restaurant and then twisted her head, looking imploringly at Gil. But he was staring at her in amazement, a grin beginning to form on his handsome face, and she knew at once what he was thinking.

"Please," she began desperately. "Gil — don't go." And Lukas turned, hesitated for a moment, then inclined his head.

"No, don't go. Come in and help us celebrate. After all, it's not every day a man gets engaged, and with something like this to celebrate we must have as many people as we can to the party!" His smile held a challenge and Alix was reminded suddenly of a stag, ready to lock antlers with its rival.

"Engaged?" Gil echoed in astonishment, and Alix closed her eyes and groaned. And then snapped them open again at the sound of the cheers issuing from the taverna.

By now, Lukas had dragged her past all the tables and into the dining room. And to her utter dismay, Alix saw that it was laid out for a party. The tables had been pushed together and were covered with white cloths. Vases of flowers and bowls of fruit stood on them, and from the ceiling floated bunches of balloons with streamers floating in the air.

"Oh, my God!" she said. *"Lukas . . ."*

But there was no time to say more. The plump woman who had served her last night was already holding her hands, smiling and laughing. She kissed Alix on the cheek and was immediately elbowed out of the way by a sturdy man who followed suit. Alix cast an agonised glance at Lukas and swore that later on she would wipe that maddening grin off his face for ever.

"My aunt Lita," he said with exaggerated formality. "And my uncle Georgio."

"My dear, we're so pleased," his aunt told her, possessing Alix's hands again and holding them in both her own. "We're very fond of Lukas, you know — we don't see nearly enough of him — and we thought that when he became betrothed and married, it would be in England. We never dreamed he'd bring his sweetheart to Crete to make the announcement. So romantic! And my mother, she's so happy for you both. She knows already that you're ideally matched."

Ideally matched? Alix swallowed hard to keep back the words that sprang to her lips. I'd sooner be matched to a cobra, she thought, taking the opportunity as his aunt turned away to give Lukas a murderous glare. Oh, why had he done this? And where was Gil?

The Englishman was at her side. "My," he murmured in her ear, "that was some whirlwind romance. You didn't even know the man last night! Or was that just an act?"

She shook her head blindly. Suddenly, he was her only friend, the one rock of sanity in this whole crazy turmoil. "Gil — I must talk to you sometime."

"I'd like that," he said. "I'd like it very much. In fact, I think I shall insist." His eyes were gleaming. "A whirlwind romance! What a story!" He smiled at her and then bent and planted a light kiss in the corner of her mouth. "What a fast worker you are," he whispered, and slid away.

Alix felt a hand on her wrist and looked up to find Lukas's dark eyes fixed upon her. For a moment, she felt as guilty as if they had been really engaged and she had been caught flirting with some other man. Then she shook herself. It was all a charade. Not real at all. And her relationships with other men were nothing to do with Lukas — why, she could go to bed with Gil if she wanted to, and he wouldn't have the right to say a word about it.

But she didn't want to go to bed with Gil. And as she stood staring up into the dark face she felt a surge of excitement. That damned aura, or scent, or whatever it is, she thought in exasperation, and tried to pull her arm away.

Lukas bent very close — far too close — and brushed his lips against her ear. A shiver ran down her entire body. She heard his voice, no more than a whisper, like brown silk being drawn softly across a polished floor.

"Don't pull away, my sweet," he murmured, and she felt the warmth of his breath on her neck. "We're supposed to be in love, remember? Now, look happy and come and sit with me at our places. My uncle wants to propose a toast."

"Why the hell are you doing this?" she muttered back. "This afternoon was bad enough but all *this* —" She gestured at the tables, laid out almost as if for a wedding, at the people — friends and family, she supposed — who all stood about, beaming, each holding a glass and lifting it towards them.

Lukas grinned. "It came as much of a shock to me as to you," he admitted. "I hadn't intended our news to travel so fast, or to have such an effect. But you know what families are — the favourite son producing a beautiful bride, the prospect of grandchildren —" He laughed outright at her scandalised expression. "Oh, Alix, your poor bewildered face! You look as if one of the tables had suddenly begun to walk. Is it so very bad — an engagement party?"

"It is when there's no engagement," she snapped. "Lukas, I can't believe you're doing this to me. Whatever possessed you to let this happen?"

"But I didn't know it was happening," he protested, looking injured. "Truly, Alix, I had no idea. My uncle and aunt arranged it all, as soon as my grandmother told them the news —"

"You surely don't expect me to believe that!" she broke in. "Why, we left her up at the old monastery — it took us nearly an hour to walk back. How could she possibly have got the news to them so soon? Is there a bush telegraph on Crete? Or maybe you just rely on good old-fashioned telepathy."

"The good old-fashioned telephone, actually," he said mildly. "My grandmother likes to live quietly in a secluded spot, but that doesn't mean we leave her totally isolated. Or perhaps you didn't notice the phone during your investigation of her home?"

Alix flushed. "Obviously my investigation, as you call it, wasn't as thorough as you imagined. No, I didn't notice it. So you're telling me that she was on the phone as soon as we were out of sight, and your aunt immediately gathered the entire clan — which looks like most of Crete — here to celebrate. Why the rush, Lukas? Why all the panic? Do they think the engagement won't last long enough to plan a party properly? Or are they just so delighted to be getting you off their hands at last that they're determined to make sure you won't even try to get out of it."

"Why," he asked gently, "do you suppose they should expect me to *want* to get out of it?"

Alix stared at him. Suddenly the whole thing was too much for her. Baffled and confused, she turned away, staring bleakly at the colourful room, at the decorations and balloons, the gaily-set tables, the laughing, chattering people.

"I don't want this," she stated. "It was bad enough this afternoon, when it was just your grandmother. But this is going too far. I'm sorry, Lukas, you're going to have to tell them."

He shook his head. "You can see how impossible it is to do that. No, I'm sorry, my sweet, but we'll just have to go along with it. We can't disappoint everyone now."

"So when *can* we disappoint them?" she enquired softly, and wished she had the courage to pull away from him and simply walk out, leaving him to make the explanations. But she couldn't do it. She had never been able to make scenes in public — that was what had made that last evening at the Minos, with Rick, so unbearable. And after all, there would have to be an end to this soon. Even Lukas wouldn't go to the lengths of marrying her, just to please his family.

And somewhere, at the back of all this, was Iphigenia. And an old man, too ill to make his search for himself, who yearned for news of the sweetheart who had been first given to him and then taken away by the war which had torn the island fifty years ago.

What was an engagement that was no more than a misunderstanding, compared with what those two lovers had endured?

Chapter Six

For any other girl, such an engagement party would have been one of the highlights of her life, a memory to be treasured. A brilliant kaleidoscope of colour, with the guests decked out in their finest traditional costume, an array of wonderful Greek dishes on the tables — not one of them chalked up on the blackboard, Alix thought as she nibbled half-heartedly at the delicious food — toasts which she could not understand but which drew both laughter and tears from her companions and, when the meal had been cleared away, Greek music and dancing which went on late into the night.

"What is he saying?" she muttered to Lukas as yet another of his innumerable uncles rose to his feet for yet another speech. Lukas was chuckling and shaking his head, and the rest of them were roaring with laughter. "For goodness' sake, Lukas, I don't understand a word!"

He looked down at her, his face alight with amusement, and she realised suddenly how very attractive he was with all the stern anger erased. His brown eyes sparkled as they met hers and his lips were parted to reveal his white teeth. The two front ones were a little crooked, their slight misalignment only making his smile all the more devastating. She stared at him, thinking of those lips on hers, and a flame licked along her veins.

"Not here," he whispered, as if he'd read her thoughts. "Later . . . hmm?"

"Not at all!" she hissed. "Just tell me what they're saying that's causing such hilarity."

"Oh, my uncle is just relating a few stories of my boyhood, to embarrass me and please everyone else. He lived with us for a while, you see, and —"

"I thought you said you grew up in London!"

He lifted one eyebrow. "There's room for more than one Greek family in London. My uncle stayed with us when he first came over to England. Then he came back to Crete, married and brought his bride over. They run our restaurant in Hampstead." He lowered the brow. "Did you think I'd been lying to you?"

"Why not?" she retorted crisply. "You've lied to your own grandmother."

There was a slight pause and for a moment she feared she had gone too far. Then Lukas said quietly, "I am no more happy about that than you are, my dear Alix. But I saw no other course open to me, to save her feelings."

"To save your own reputation, you mean."

He looked at her consideringly, then said, "There was more than that involved. But I can hardly expect you to understand that."

No, you can't, Alix thought, but there was a

sting in his words that made her think there was something else behind them. His smile had disappeared and for a moment she saw again the hard, angry expression she had come to associate with him. Baffled, she turned away, then remembered something and turned back.

"You said your uncle runs the restaurant in Hampstead. Does that mean your family owns more than one?"

"Clever girl," he said with sarcastic admiration, and she bit her lip in annoyance for giving him the opportunity. "Yes, as a matter of fact we own several. Three in London, one in York, one in Bath —"

"All the prime tourist spots," she said, trying to equal his sarcasm with her own.

"Naturally. It's a business. One sets up one's business where it is likely to do best." His uncle had stopped speaking now and an expectant silence fell. Everyone's eyes turned towards them in anticipation, and Lukas rose gracefully to his feet.

Once again, Alix was forced to sit through a torrent of incomprehensible Greek. But if she couldn't understand the words, Lukas's actions were making his meaning all too clear. He was thanking everyone for having come — at such short notice, he added, making them all laugh. He was telling them about Alix, how lovely she was — his fingers touched her face and hair lightly, as if showing off some prize acquisition, she thought — and what a lucky man he was to

118

have found her. Approving nods and smiles all round, especially from the men. Then he appeared to embark on a long story to which they all listened with interest, ending on a note of triumph which brought cheers and actual applause. Last of all, he held out his own glass, first towards Alix, to which they all responded with enthusiasm, and then to the company at large.

"Lift your glass," he whispered to her as she hesitated. "We're toasting my family and friends." And hastily, desperate not to cause any offence to these good people, who were all being so deceived, she did so.

Lukas sat down, to the sound of more applause, and the younger men present all leapt up and began to clear the tables and move them aside to make space for the dancing.

"What were you telling them?" Alix demanded.

Lukas smiled. "Oh, how we met, how at first you tossed your head and took little notice of me, how I pursued you with flowers and chocolates until at last you agreed to come out with me, how our courtship —"

"Our *what?* You told them all that?" She stared at him. "You made up all those lies, on the spur of the moment?"

"Oh, it was easy enough," he said modestly. "I just remembered the stories in the women's magazines my mother reads and —"

"I'm not *congratulating* you!" she exploded.

"I'm appalled. That you could stand up in front of all your family —"

"Not all of them. My mother and father are still in —"

"— and tell them that . . . that . . . that *fandango* of lies —" She stopped. Lukas had flung back his head and let out a peal of laughter. It rang through the room and Alix realised that everyone had stopped what they were doing to look in his direction and smile. Her face flaming, she slapped at the nearest portion of him, which happened to be his arm, and there was a general chuckle. Obviously everyone thought he was teasing her about something and she was punishing him with a playful smack.

Playful! There'll be nothing playful about it when I get you alone, she thought, and then felt more hot colour run up into her face. Wasn't *alone* with him the last place she wanted to find herself?

"I think you mean *farrago* of lies," Lukas said, getting his face back together. "A *fandango* is a dance."

"I know that," she snapped. "And that's what I said. Farrago, I mean —" as his face started to crack again. "Oh, what does it matter anyway? You know what I'm talking about. I'm just appalled at all the lies you've just told. It was bad enough this afternoon, when it was just your grandmother, but now it seems like half the island. How many people *are* you related to, for goodness' sake?"

"Oh, quite a few," he said airily. "And what else could I do? This is an engagement party, no one's met or even heard of you before, they all expect to be told our story."

"We don't *have* a story!"

"Well, we're rapidly developing one. I could hardly stand up and say, it was like this, my bride —"

"I'm not your bride! I'm never going to be —"

"— used to come into my restaurant," he continued as if she had not spoken, "but then we didn't meet again until yesterday, when she clearly didn't recognise me, and then again this afternoon when I found her burgling my grand-mother's —"

"I *wasn't!* You know I wasn't."

"— and I suddenly realised I couldn't live without her, so dreamed up this engagement —"

"This *blackmail* —"

"— so that she wouldn't be able to get away until she knew she loved me too," he finished dramatically. But his eyes were suddenly serious, and as Alix looked into them she felt a strange quiver deep inside. For a moment she had the wild, incredible feeling that it was almost as if he meant it . . . But no. That wasn't love she saw there, it was menace. A dark warning. If she didn't go along with him . . .

Alix shuddered. If she didn't go along with him now, her position in Plakias, and probably the whole of the Rethymnon area, would be impossible. Her quest for Iphigenia would be doomed. Not a soul would help her if she broke away from Lukas after tonight, when she had been welcomed into their midst with such warm generosity, with such unquestioning acceptance. She might as well get on the next plane and go back to London.

Which is just what I'd like to do, she thought, crossing her arms over her breasts. And would do, if it weren't for my promise to Grandfather.

"You're cold," Lukas said with all the solicitude that might be expected from a newly-engaged man. "Here, let me warm you." He slipped his arm about her shoulders and her nerves jumped. "Mm, that's nice," he murmured. "You fit there very well, don't you think?"

Alix had to admit that she did. His arm was large and strong, warm against the bare skin at the back of her neck and shoulders. Immediately, she wished she had worn a high-necked, long-sleeved pullover instead of the scoop-necked blouse. She could feel his fingers touching her upper arm, moving in slow, gentle circles, and she fought the impulse to close her eyes and lean back against his body.

A girl could feel totally safe here, she thought. Totally protected. *If* she knew he loved her — and if she loved him.

But Lukas didn't love her. And she was just about as safe here as she would have been in a tiger's lair, curled up amongst the cubs.

There was nothing she could do, however, but

endure it. And soon all the tables had been cleared away and the men lined up around the room for the dancing.

During the whole evening, the waiters had been busily serving the normal customers who sat outside on the big covered patio. Now they were invited in too, to share in the celebrations, and they brought their chairs and squeezed around the walls, their faces alight with interest. Alix scanned them, but to her relief could see no one she knew — unsurprisingly, though it wasn't uncommon to meet acquaintances on holidays abroad, especially in a small place like Plakias. And the way things were going, she thought, it would have been just her luck to see half her friends grinning at her across the room.

It seemed that she was to be spared this embarrassment, though. The only familiar face was Gil's. He waved at her and she smiled a rather sickly smile back. Another man she'd met only a day ago — but now he seemed like a lifeline. Would he be able to help her out of this mess? And what sort of help did she need? How could anyone help, let alone a stranger she'd met only yesterday . . .

But she seemed to have got herself engaged to a stranger she'd met only yesterday . . .

The sweet, faint music of a stringed instrument penetrated her thoughts and she glanced towards the end of the room, where a man was standing, his heart-shaped instrument held upon his knee, his bow moving gently across the strings. Alix listened as the tender harmony pervaded the air, and felt a sudden piercing sense of sadness. It was as if the music were expressing her own lost emotions, as if someone she loved had stroked her heartstrings and then forsaken her.

Rick . . . ? But Rick had never touched her in the way this music was touching her now. She felt Lukas's fingers, moving gently on her bare arm, moving in time to the melody, and it was if he had laid her heart bare, as if with each note he could touch her very depths.

She moved abruptly, but before either could speak the door opened and the little crowd around it parted to let a late arrival pass into the big room.

Alix gasped. The newcomer was tall, his height accentuated by his high, black headgear. His face was almost hidden by a huge, bushy grey beard, and he wore a black gown which swept the floor.

The priest.

Suddenly panic-stricken, she turned swiftly to Lukas and surprised a look on his face almost as disconcerted as her own. Then he gave her a quick, reassuring grin.

"It's all right. He hasn't come to marry us. Only to bless us."

"To *bless* us? But —"

"It's customary at the engagement party. Of course, this isn't quite the usual kind of engagement —"

"I should think not," she said sardonically. "Usually, the happy couple would have met and fallen in love some time earlier, I should imagine."

"Now, there," Lukas said earnestly, as if starting a lesson on Cretan folk customs, "you'd be wrong. In earlier times, it was quite common for the man and woman never to have set eyes on each other until the formal betrothal. These days, of course, things are more relaxed — they might have seen each other at a feast or something of the kind and indicated to their parents that they're interested. Or perhaps the families themselves have made the decision. At any rate, the couple themselves are supposed to know nothing at all about the negotiations that are carried out while each family investigates the credentials — and wealth — of the other and the marriage contract is drawn up. Indeed —"

"*Lukas!*" she hissed. "Will you please stop chattering and tell this priest that he *can't* bless us! It's impossible."

"Impossible?" he said. "But why?"

"You know perfectly well why. Because we're not getting engaged — not really. It's all a charade. You know it is. And I can't let a priest bless me — in front of all these people — and know I'm telling lies." She could see the priest approaching, his tall black figure exuding authority, intimidating despite the friendly smile behind his beard. "Look," she said rapidly, "I've gone along with all this up to now but this is as

125

far as I'm prepared to go. I will not tell lies to a priest."

"He's a Christian priest. You're not joining some foreign sect."

"That's not the point. It doesn't matter what my religion is, or even if I *have* a religion. It's an offence to do something all these people believe in and hold dear. And I won't do it."

She looked him in the eye. There was no vacillating on this one — no giving way to a personality that threatened to sweep her away with it. Nor any sexual *frisson*.

Lukas stared at her for a long moment. There was an odd expression in his eyes, as if he had asked himself a casual question and been answered with something more solemn. He glanced aside to see where the priest was, and then took her hands.

Alix saw that the priest had been waylaid by a group of Lukas's relatives, all talking with animation. Probably fixing the wedding date, she thought, and felt her heart sink. How were all these people going to react when they discovered the truth?

"Alix, listen to me," Lukas said, and she realised he had been talking for several seconds. "We won't be telling any lies. We won't be making any vows. All we need do is let him lay his hands on our heads and wish us well in our future lives. The fact that we won't be spending them together doesn't enter into it. And nobody will be hurt or upset. We can break the engagement later — I've told you, I'll do it gently in a few weeks' time — and everyone will be sorry, but that's all." He kept his eyes on her face. "Is it really so much better to create a scene here and now, when everyone's having a good time, than to let the news filter through gradually later on, when they're busy with other things?"

Create a scene . . . Alix's whole nature revolted at the idea. And she was struck by the parallel. Her last engagement had ended in a Greek restaurant — Lukas's own restaurant, in London. That had been painful enough, but this would be much, much worse. Could she face it?

She looked up at him, her eyes filled with uncertainty.

"You promise we won't have to say anything? And even if we don't, we're not letting *him* say things that aren't true?"

"There will be no lies," he said gravely. "Look, Alix, I'm no happier than you are about this. This whole party — it wasn't my idea. The preparations were under way before I even got back to the taverna. There really was nothing I could do about it. As for the priest, well, I'm as surprised as you. I just hadn't thought about this at all."

Alix looked into his eyes and saw what she could have sworn was complete sincerity. Was it true? Had the whole thing just got out of hand? But she'd been equally certain, only a few minutes ago, that he was enjoying the proceedings immensely.

And why not? she thought sourly. The joke was at her expense, not his.

"Go along with it, just for now. Please," he said, and she followed the direction of his glance across the room and saw his grandmother.

She had been there all evening, sitting at the head of the long table in a high-backed wooden armchair obviously brought specially in her honour from someone's home. Every time Alix had glanced her way, she had smiled and nodded, lifting her glass in a silent toast.

Now she was watching the priest as he made his way across the room. He had already stopped to speak to her, laying his hands on hers, and Alix had seen the expression on her face as she gazed up at him, speaking softly. That same expression was there now — a mingling of pride, happiness and love. It was directed towards Lukas — and towards Alix herself.

I can't, she thought. I can't say the words that will kill that expression for ever, and might even kill the old lady too.

Lukas rose to his feet and drew her up beside him. They faced the priest together and slowly bowed their heads.

After that solemn moment, the party started again with renewed vigour. The music of the lyre began again, accompanied on a flute by one of Lukas's uncles — was there any man here who wasn't an uncle or a cousin? Alix wondered — and together they played a slow but rhythmic melody that started everyone clapping, while the men got to their feet and formed a long line at one side of the room, facing Alix and Lukas. They laid their arms across each other's shoulders and began to dance, slowly at first and then, as the music quickened, more rapidly, their steps perfectly in time. As they danced, they moved across the floor until they were directly in front of the couple whose engagement they were celebrating, and then several of them leaned down and caught Lukas by the shoulders, yanking him to his feet.

Lukas laughed and went with them, taking the place of honour in the centre of the line. Fascinated, Alix watched as he matched their nimble steps, moving first one way and then the other, the line so closely interwoven that it seemed almost to take shape as one cohesive being, twining its way from end to end of the long room, twisting like a giant snake yet without ever missing a beat of the insistent rhythm of the music.

Almost abruptly, the music ceased and the line fell away, leaving Lukas on his own in the middle of the floor. For a moment or two he stood perfectly still in the silence. And then the lyre and flute began again.

The melody was soft and haunting at first, and Lukas's steps slow and delicate. Then the strains began to rise, so that he moved more quickly, his feet skipping rapidly to keep up. The musicians watched him intently as they played, still increasing their speed, and his steps became yet more intricate to match the complexity of the tune. The audience, which had begun clapping softly the moment the dance had begun, now clapped faster and louder, emphasising a beat which seemed to strike directly into Alix's breast.

She leaned forward, totally caught up in the powerful music and the vigour of the man who danced before her. His feet flashed, now almost too fast to follow, and as he kicked and leapt he looked straight into Alix's eyes. This was a dance of commitment, she realised suddenly, a dance in which a young man would declare his love for his betrothed wife, with which he promised her marriage, children, a life together . . .

Entranced, she watched, unable to take her eyes from the leaping figure. There was nothing effeminate in this dance, nothing conciliatory. This was a dance of power, of virility, of masculine pride and authority. A man who could dance like this could do anything — *would* do anything — to protect what was his. Fight to the death — match hate with hate, love with love — and never, never surrender.

The Cretans had been invaded during the war. But they had not surrendered. Occupied by the enemy, they had nevertheless resisted, every man, woman and child. They had never given in.

Alix felt a shiver of apprehension. How had she come to be involved with such a man, in such an intimate way? And what would happen if — *when* — she decided that enough really was enough, and turned to walk away?

The music rose in a crescendo and Lukas matched it with a whirling leap that took him higher than any other. He landed on both feet, exactly as the two musicians came to their final, climactic note, stood perfectly still for a moment, then bowed deeply first to Alix and then to the audience.

There was a moment of silence before the applause began, and then everyone began to clap and cheer. Some stamped their feet and the men whistled. Lukas grinned and ran his fingers through his hair, and then held his hand out to Alix.

"Oh!" she gasped, realising he wanted her to join him on the floor. "No, I can't!" But he laughed and insisted, and she felt hands on her back, urging her forwards. The whole crowd was laughing and encouraging her and, with the feeling that she had no choice, would probably never have any choice again, she stood up and went hesitantly out into what now seemed a vast empty space.

Lukas took both her hands and drew her close. She looked up at him imploringly. His eyes were very dark and there was a softness about his mouth she hadn't noticed before. His chest rose and fell quickly, as if he were still breathless from his dance.

The music began again.

"No!" she whispered, panic-stricken. "I can't! I *can't* dance."

"Of course you can." He gathered both her hands against his chest. "Every holidaymaker does. And you needn't do it alone. Everyone else will join in."

Alix cast an anguished glance about the room. No one had moved. They were all watching, smiling but intent. She saw the grandmother's face, nodding encouragement.

Lukas laid his arm across her shoulder and began to move.

"Just follow my steps."

There was nothing else to be done. Feeling that by now nothing she did mattered anyway, Alix looked down at his feet and moved her own in imitation. One to the side, cross the other in front, one to the side, cross the other behind. It was easy enough, after all. Side, cross, side, cross . . . The music played slowly, softly, not increasing in speed as it had before. Side, cross, side, cross . . .

She felt someone on her other side, laying another arm across her shoulders, and glanced up to find Lukas's uncle Georgio looking kindly down at her. Alix smiled back, missed a step and hastily returned her concentration to her feet. Side, cross, side, cross . . .

Now the others began to join in, extending the line in both directions so that she and Lukas remained always in the centre. They moved backwards and forwards along the room, swaying to the gentle rhythm. And, to her surprise, Alix found she was beginning to enjoy herself. After all, she thought dreamily, it was a wonderful party. It would be crazy not to get *something* out of this impossible situation.

She scarcely noticed when the music began to quicken. She only knew that suddenly she was skipping and leaping with the rest of them, her feet following the dance effortlessly, as if the entire rhythm, the whole sequence of movements were something they had learned long ago. As if it matched some deep primeval urge, as if it were as natural as living itself.

But there was no time to think. With everyone else she was swept up in the passion and vigour of the dance, the long line prancing now like a multi-headed animal with its own corporate responses. Twisting, leaping, gyrating, they wound themselves about the room until suddenly, as if at some unspoken command, they separated and each person danced alone, flinging out arms and legs, clapping and spinning, the music leading them as if by an unseen cord, the rhythm too insistent to ignore, too powerful to mistake.

Alix found herself facing another of Lukas's uncles. He was short and fat but he stamped and jumped as energetically as any of them. He grinned broadly at her, and she laughed back, feeling a warmth she had not known since she was in New Zealand with her grandfather.

Her grandfather! He had been here, he might have met some of these people. That old man in the corner, the ancient woman sitting by the door — they might have known him. They must have known Iphigenia.

I'll ask them, she thought with sudden determination. But her thoughts could go no further, for Lukas was beside her again, his arm firmly about her waist, and they were now dancing as a couple, to music that had slowed and changed its metre. A waltz, she thought with surprise, and found herself in Lukas's arms, their feet moving smoothly in unison.

"In your honour," he murmured, his lips touching her ear. "You've done so well in our dancing, now it's time to pay our respects by playing something you will recognise."

"And suppose I hadn't been able to waltz?" she enquired, trying to control the sudden kicking of her heart. "I might have been able only to do disco-dancing."

"Then the musicians would quickly have changed their tune." He waited a moment, then added casually, "As you might do yourself, perhaps."

Alix turned her head to stare at him, baffled. Their eyes met and once again her heart jumped as she realised how very close he was, close enough to feel his breath on her skin, close enough to feel his lips on her cheek . . . Abruptly, she turned away again.

"I don't know what you mean," she said shakily.

"I mean this search for Iphigenia, of course," he said, and his voice was suddenly hard again.

"Give it up, Alix. It's a hopeless quest and will do no one any good."

"Why not?" she demanded, still following him in the dance. "And what business is it of yours, anyway?"

"That's not important —"

"Isn't it? You interfere with my business, you set the village men against me in Sellia, and you say it's not important? I think it's very important indeed." She turned again to meet his dark brown eyes. "And I might remind you, Lukas, that you promised to help me in return for — for all this." She released her hand from his and waved it at the throng who were now trying with varying degrees of success to match the steps of the waltz.

"Well, not quite all this," he said, repossessing her hand. "This, I hadn't anticipated. I'm not going back on my promise, Alix. I simply wanted to suggest that you might see sense and —"

"And nothing," she retorted crisply. "I'll do what I came here to do — with or without your help."

Lukas hesitated for a second, then shrugged. "Very well. And now, Alix, smile at me. You've been glowering like a sulky schoolgirl for the past five minutes. We don't want people to think we're having our first quarrel, do we?"

Don't we? Alix thought, attracted by the idea. Wouldn't it be the best way out of this mess? But then Lukas wouldn't help her find Iphigenia, and she knew she needed his help. A blazing row here on the dance floor, at their own engagement party, wasn't going to gain her the sympathy of the islanders.

Obediently, she bared her teeth at Lukas, and he laughed and kissed her. "You look like a savage little kitten. A ginger kitten," he added, running his fingers over her chestnut hair. "Now, behave yourself. Cuddle up close and look as if you can't wait to get married!"

"You're not being fair," she muttered as he tightened his arms about her, compelling her to obey. "You're taking advantage of the situation." She was acutely aware of his body against hers, of the shape and strength of him. Her own strength seemed to have deserted her, leaving her knees weak and trembling, her body dependent on Lukas's arms. She felt her blood tingle and shivered, knowing that he must feel every slightest tremor.

"Not cold again?" he murmured. His lips were touching her hair, her ears, her neck. She felt the fire of his tongue, its tip gently grazing her skin, exploring the tiny crevices, stroking the smooth softness. His arms were holding her so close that they seemed to have wrapped themselves twice about her slender body and, as the music swelled and softened about them, it was as if he lifted her on to a silken cloud, so that her feet moved without effort, without sensation; as if there were no one else in the room but the two of them; as if they had floated out through walls that melted before them, and now drifted somewhere amongst the stars . . .

As gently as a sigh, the music ended. Alix felt herself lowered lightly to the floor, and stood for a moment in the circle of Lukas's arms, still in thrall to the plaintive harmony, as bemused as if she had indeed just descended from the stars.

She looked up into his face. The room was totally silent, as if everyone held their breath and waited. Lukas looked down at her, his eyes once more almost black, with only that glittering rim of bronze, and then, slowly, he bent his head and took her lips with his.

Chapter Seven

Sunlight was flooding into the bedroom when Alix stirred next morning. Or was it afternoon? she pondered, wincing as a dull pain throbbed through her head.

Oh, *no* — a hangover! And was it any wonder? Her glass had been filled over and over again for the interminable toasts, until she had lost count and was, anyway, past caring. The evening had swept along like a torrent, taking her with it like a leaf tossed in a cascade, and she had had no choice but to swim with the stream, clinging to Lukas as if to a lifeline and hoping that eventually it would end and she might be washed up in some sandy cove while the rest of the flood surged on without her.

She lay still, trying to recall the events of last night. The party had gone on until the small hours of the morning — indeed, it was almost dawn when Lukas had finally brought her back to her apartment. After the waltz and the long, lingering kiss which had left her trembling and almost brought the house down, the music had started again, once more swinging into the lively music of the island, and everyone had begun to dance again. All the old traditional dances were displayed for her, from the *syrto,* a measured and stately line dance from the Heraklion region, to the local *pedetko,* which gave the men another chance to show off their wild leaps, and then the jigging gaiety of the *pentazole.*

And when the dancers were exhausted, the singers took over. Alix felt the tears in her eyes as she listened to the soulful voices, telling a wistful story in liquid melody. She needed little translation to know the theme of their song, but Lukas bent towards her and whispered in her ear.

"This is a *mandinade* — a traditional song in rhyming couplets. It tells the story of a couple unlucky in love. They want each other but can't admit it — their families stand in the way, for they've feuded for generations and if these two were to acknowledge their love openly a terrible vendetta would break out. There is nothing left for them but to commit suicide, for without each other they cannot live."

Alix stared at him. "That's the story of Romeo and Juliet!"

He smiled at her. "A common enough tale in many countries, I imagine."

"Does . . . does it still happen today?" she asked, not sure if she wanted to hear the answer.

Lukas shrugged. "Who knows what goes on in these traditional cultures?"

You know, she thought, but you don't intend to say. Not to me — an outsider. And she felt suddenly cold, as if she had been slapped.

The song had changed to one more cheerful,

and then to another which was joined by several other singers and brought much laughter. The company began to look at Lukas and Alix again, and the singers beckoned and encouraged him to join them. Not me! Alix thought, shrinking back in her seat as he rose to his feet, but it seemed that this time she was not required. She watched as he crossed the floor, and caught her breath as he began to sing.

His voice filled the room. It was a deep baritone, soaring to the roof and making the fabric of the entire building tremble. He sang with power and vigour, letting his voice pour forth at full strength; but when the song ended, it had softened to a caress.

Again, there was a tiny silence before the applause began. Alix found herself clapping as wildly as the rest, and knew that Lukas had seen her. But the performance had been so astonishing, it would have been petty to withhold her appreciation. She smiled across the room at him, holding up her hands as she clapped them together.

The singers began again, returning to the form which had brought so much laughter, singing a bar or two each as if having a conversation. And that's just what it was, Alix suddenly realised as Lukas joined in. A quick-fire, witty conversation — and slightly risqué, too, she judged from the tone of the laughter. She saw people looking her way as they laughed, and her face burned as it dawned on her that the repartee now concerned her and Lukas. Were they making it up as they went along? And what were they saying? What was *Lukas* saying?

"It would take forever to tell you," he said, laughing as he came back to his seat. "You'll have to learn Greek. But it was only harmless banter."

Harmless banter that compounds our lies even further, she thought, but she was too tired now to start another argument. She accepted another drink and sagged a little, wondering how much longer the party would go on. Lukas slipped his arm about her.

"You're worn out." He sounded truly solicitous now, rather than as if he were putting on a performance as he had done earlier. "Lean against me."

She had done so, feeling grateful despite herself, and there she had sat watching the rest of the dancing, listening to the singing and smiling sleepily at the well-wishers who formed a constant procession to their table. With Lukas's arm about her, she had felt safe, secure, and although her brain tried to tell her this was an illusion, she was too weary and too bemused to take notice of its warnings. Tomorrow, she thought, I'll worry about it tomorrow . . .

And now tomorrow was here. The party had ended at last and Lukas had walked her the short distance to her apartment. Dawn was beginning to shade the sky with apricot, the shapes of the mountains were dark against the lightened sky and in the olive trees the first birds were beginning to sing.

He had stopped at her apartment door and Alix had fumbled with her key. Suddenly uncertain, she lifted her eyes to his. How did you say goodnight to a man to whom you had just announced your engagement in front of half of Crete? How did you say goodnight, when you knew it was all a sham?

Lukas seemed to know. He bent and brushed her forehead lightly with his lips. He touched her face with his fingertips and then stepped back.

"Goodnight, Alix," he said quietly, and there was an odd huskiness in his voice. "Sleep well. I'll call for you in the morning." He gave a brief, half-rueful grin as he glanced at the rosy sky. "Or should I simply say 'later on'?"

He turned and walked quickly away. And Alix had watched him out of sight before turning and going into the suddenly cold and lonely apartment.

With a swift movement, Alix swung her legs over the side of the bed and stood up. The sheet dropped away, leaving her body naked, and she walked through to the shower room and turned on the spray. It hit her full on her breasts, and she gasped with shock.

She had totally forgotten that it was likely to be cold! Like so many of the small apartments and hotels, the water was heated by solar panels, and often used up by the time everyone had taken their evening shower. There was seldom hot water in the mornings. For a few seconds, the water felt icy as it streamed down over her body, and then she began to get accustomed to it, and even enjoy it. Perhaps it was just what she needed, she thought, braving it long enough to smother her skin with gel and rub it into a soft lather. And as she stepped out a few moments later and wrapped herself in a large bath sheet, she had to admit that she felt refreshed.

A cup of strong coffee banished the rest of her headache, and she looked at her watch and tried to remember what Lukas had said before he left her. He would call for her later — but what time? It was now almost noon. He could be here at any minute.

And find me in nothing but a towel? she thought, and began feverishly to drag clothes out of the wardrobe. What should she wear? Where would he be taking her? She still wasn't quite sure whether trousers gave offence. Not in the towns and holiday resorts, perhaps, but suppose they went to some tiny village where visitors rarely penetrated? She chose a sarong-style skirt in a mixture of orange and terracotta colours, and added a plain blouse in the same shade of terracotta.

She took a second cup of coffee out on to the little patch of grass and sat at the small table under the olive tree. The water of the bay was glittering with tiny wavelets, each topped with a crest of shimmering foam. A fishing boat was steadily plying its way back to the harbour and near at hand a pair of goldfinches flitted between the trees. An old man walked slowly past, giving her a cheerful wave, and she smiled back.

Was Lukas coming? she wondered. And did she really want him to come, anyway? What was their expedition likely to achieve?

Find Iphigenia, she hoped. That was what it was all about, wasn't it? But did Lukas really intend to help her?

She remembered how hostile he had been at the taverna in Sellia yesterday. How his eyes had hardened when she showed him her grandfather's sketch, how abruptly he had told her that Iphigenia had gone. *None of these men remember her,* he had said — yet how could he know? *You might as well give up and go home.*

And then, only a few hours later, he had struck a bargain with her. Go along with their sham engagement, and he would help her find the old woman. Did his good name mean so much to him that he was prepared to retract his earlier antagonism? And what had caused that antagonism in the first place?

Or had he not retracted at all? Did he mean simply to keep her occupied, so that she had no time to continue her search?

She thought again of the party last night. There had been moments when she had seen another side of Lukas. Moments when his face had softened as he talked to his grandmother, when he had shown Alix herself an unexpected tenderness, when his hands and voice had been gentle. And there had been moments when, watching him leap in his solo dance or listening to his rich baritone voice, she had felt a warmth towards him that grew when he had taken her in his arms for the waltz. A warmth that in other circumstances she might have described as love.

Love. Ridiculous! She was no more likely to fall in love with Lukas than to fly to Mars. Nor he with her. No, it was that wretched aura of his, that palpable sexuality that seemed to exude from every pore and which, unexpectedly and most unfortunately, seemed to strike an immediate response in her. She'd heard of such things and scoffed at them. Love at first sight, she supposed it was called, which really meant a sexual attraction at first sight. Love itself came later, when a couple had had time to get to know one another, when they could be sure that their values and attitudes chimed in harmony.

There was no chance of her values coming within a mile of his. Lies to grandmothers! Parties to celebrate engagements that didn't exist! No way.

All the same, she was involved in those very lies, and while the knowledge made her squirm with shame, she knew that since the situation existed she would make sure that Lukas carried out his part of the bargain, and helped her find Iphigenia.

Which meant that she had to spend time with him. And his aura.

Oh *hell!* Alix thought crossly. And the worst of it is, he's all too well aware of it and not at all above taking advantage of it. And she wondered yet again whether she was wise in going with him to heaven knew where.

Well, that was the argument back full circle. She took a deep draught of coffee and prepared to start again, with no real hope of coming to a better conclusion.

Her thoughts were interrupted by the arrival of a car. It was small and red and she glanced at it without interest, her eyes widening as the door opened and Lukas unfolded his long, lean body from the driver's seat.

"Good morning," he greeted her cheerfully. "Up bright and early, I see. How are you feeling?"

"I'm all right, thanks," Alix answered cautiously. She looked at the car. "Is . . . is that yours?"

He shook his head. "My aunt's. It's a little on the small side for me — I need a shoehorn to get me into it. But it's better than borrowing the family donkey."

Alix stared at him and then laughed suddenly at the picture of the two of them riding in tandem on one of the donkeys she had seen ambling around the roads. Lukas grinned back at her and sat down in the chair opposite.

"Any more coffee going?" He indicated her cup and Alix got up before she could stop herself and went into the apartment. Once there, she halted. What was she doing, waiting on him? Was this how Cretan wives and fiancées behaved? All the same, she found herself spooning coffee into a mug and filling it with boiling water. She carried it out to him.

"There's only black — I've run out of milk."

"That's fine." He took it, his fingers touching hers as he did so, and she felt the now familiar fire run its thin tongue up her arm. She snatched her hand away, jerking the mug so that some of the coffee spilled on to the table, making a black pool on the green surface. Clicking her tongue in annoyance, she went back inside to fetch a cloth.

"How very domestic," he drawled, his eyes glinting. "You'll make someone a good wife one of these days."

"Not you, that's for sure," Alix snarled, her momentary good temper dissipated. She saw his brows lift and bit her lip, ashamed of her surliness, then decided that it might be just as well to stay that way. Anything that served to keep his mind off her body — and hers off his.

"Well, well, all in good time," he said comfortably. He sipped his coffee and gazed at the view. "Pleasant spot, isn't it? I could sit here all day."

"Don't even think of it," she advised him. "You're going to help me find Iphigenia, remember? Or has last night's party blotted it all from your mind?"

"It was a good evening, wasn't it?" he said reminiscently. "But no, I don't think anything has been expunged from my memory. Just one small correction, though — I agreed to help you *look for* Iphigenia. Not necessarily find her. I fear that might be beyond even my virtually unlimited powers."

Alix stared at him. "You have a very good opinion of yourself."

Lukas laughed. "Oh, come on, Alix, let your face crack a little. That was a joke. You've met jokes before, surely? Funny things, you know?"

"You're the funniest joke I've met," she said. "Unfortunately, all jokes pall eventually."

"Depends on your sense of humour, I suppose," he said equably. "Well, what do you suggest we do now? I am at your disposal." He waved his arm with a large gesture of munificence.

"What do *I* suggest we do now?" Alix repeated. "How do I know? You're the one who's supposed to be helping."

"But how can I help you if I don't know what you're trying to do? Oh, I know you're trying to find this person — but what clues do you have? She's an old woman now, you told them that at the taverna, but just how old? And just why are you trying to find her anyway?"

There was a sudden tension in his voice as he spoke the last words, and Alix knew this was the crucial question. Why was she trying to find Iphigenia? He was leaning forward slightly, his brows drawn together, his eyes narrowed. He had asked the question before, and it was clear that he meant to have an answer this time.

She debated within herself. Should she tell him? But again her grandfather's warning came into her mind, and with it the dread word *vendetta*. She thought of Lukas's reaction yesterday when he had seen the sketch. She remembered his accusations — the insinuation that she would cause havoc in Iphigenia's life. That she had come here to harass the old woman.

In London, urbane in his city suit, and even here outside her apartment, clad in blue jeans and a red open-necked shirt, he looked as civilised as any Westerner. But last night she had seen a different side of him — a wild, leaping Cretan with a background of tough independence and passionate love of liberty. And *vendetta*.

Looking at him now, listening to his cultured voice, it was easy enough to think of him as a product of the city. But beneath that polished veneer was he still wild enough to take the law into his own hands? To follow to the ends of the earth a man who had wronged a woman of his island? To follow such a man to New Zealand, even after fifty years had passed?

Alix shook herself. What nonsense! Of course Lukas had no such intention. He didn't even know Iphigenia — though it was clear that he knew *of* her. Or did he just want to protect an old woman from the pressures of the Western world?

Alix glanced at him and remembered another of the remarks he had made yesterday.

"But surely you know why I'm looking for

her?" she said lightly. "That's what you said yesterday, anyway. That you knew exactly why I was here, and your advice was to forget it. Are you saying now that was another lie?"

He stared at her. There was an odd expression in his eyes. If she had known him better, she might have identified it as disappointment.

"So I was right," he said heavily, and she shrugged.

"You're so certain you know, why should I argue?" That, at least, got her off the hook of having to tell him the truth. And whatever idea he'd got into his head about her, it wouldn't lead to trouble for her grandfather. She gave him a bright, sunny smile.

Lukas did not return it. Instead, he stared at the green table as if he had never seen such a thing before, his face set in hard lines. She saw again the man who had been so hostile to her in Sellia, and shivered. Had it really been necessary to waken his antagonism again?

"You promised to help me," she reminded him in a tight little voice. "I've gone along with everything, from lying to your grandmother to putting myself on display in front of half the island. You can't let me down now."

He shrugged. "Did I say I intended to? I was just reminding myself of something I should have learned long ago — not to be taken in by a pretty face. Perhaps I'd begun to hope I was wrong."

"Oh, surely not," Alix said sarcastically. "It

would be such a strange experience for you."

Lukas gave her a long look. Then he got up, so suddenly that he almost knocked over the table, and turned on his heel, taking only half a dozen swift steps to his car. Startled, Alix began to formulate a protest, but she had only the first word out of her mouth when he reached inside, pulled out a fold of paper and slammed the door again.

"This is a map of the Rethymnon area," he said curtly, laying it on the table. "Now, I've been up to Sellia this morning and made a few enquiries. It seems likely that Iphigenia — if she's the woman they remember — may have gone to live in a tiny village in the north of the region." His finger stabbed at the paper. "It's small and isolated, so if she did go there it's almost certain they'll know what happened to her."

"If anything," Alix said.

"What?" He stared at her.

"If anything at all happened to her. She might still be living there."

Lukas seemed nonplussed for a moment, then inclined his head. "Yes. I suppose she might. Well, if she is, and if she *is* the same woman, we'll find her. If not —"

"Yes?"

He shrugged. "We don't. That's all."

"Well, not quite," Alix said. "She may have moved again. In which case, we go on looking. Until we do find her."

Lukas rested his eyes on her face. Slowly, he shook his head.

"Do you know, I almost admire you. You just never let up, do you. You're determined to find this poor old body and nothing is going to stand in your way."

"That's right," Alix said coolly. "Nothing. Not even you."

Their eyes met. For a long moment, they held each other's gaze. Then Lukas turned away. He picked up his map.

"Let's get going then. The sooner this is over, the better I shall like it."

"That goes for me, too," Alix muttered as she locked the apartment door. She had already dropped some cheese and fruit into her rucksack and swung it on to her shoulder before following him to the little red car. Well, this is it, she told herself. If he has any other nefarious scheme in mind, you're putting yourself right into his hands!

The truth of this thought struck her even more forcibly as she bent to squeeze herself into the car. Even for someone small and slight, like herself, it was a squash. How Lukas had managed it was a mystery. He had given himself more leg room by pushing the seat back as far as it would go, so that he seemed almost to be sitting behind Alix, but his head was brushing the roof and his arms seemed to need an extra elbow in order to hold the steering wheel comfortably.

It would be difficult to carry out any kind of

assault in such a confined space, she thought with a blend of grim humour and thankfulness. But the trouble was, Lukas didn't need to assault her — once she got within that strange, compelling personal space of his, she was a willing accomplice. Even now, her heart was kicking and her breath coming quickly, while her face and neck felt uncomfortably hot. We're sitting far too close to each other, she thought. Did he have to bring quite such a small car?

Lukas drove with easy efficiency, apparently totally relaxed but — as Alix saw when they rounded a corner to be confronted by a flock of bleating, panic-stricken goats — ready to deal with any emergency.

He took the road out of Plakias, through the gorge which the coach had used two days earlier. Without hurry, pointing out interesting sights on the way, he could have been any local showing a tourist around. As they slowed to wend their way through the narrow streets of Mirthios, Alix ventured a question.

"You know the area very well. You must have spent a lot of time here, even though you lived in London."

"I told you, my father was very anxious to see that I knew his homeland. And naturally my family welcomed me here. The Cretans have very strong family bonds. We care about each other and we like to be sure that no one is threatened by outsiders."

Was that a warning? There was an odd note in

153

his voice, as if he were telling her something else. But Alix was determined not to be put off by hints, even when delivered by someone as dangerous to her as Lukas. She went on talking, driven by a need to find out more about this enigmatic man who seemed to think he knew so much about her.

"Your English is excellent. Didn't you find it difficult when you first started to mix with other children?"

He looked at her in astonishment. "Not at all. Why should I?"

"Well, don't you speak Greek at home? With your parents?"

"Oh, I see what you mean." He laughed. "No, my mother's British. Well, Scots, to be precise. She has the very pure speech of the Highlander. As for her Greek, hard though she tries, she's never really mastered it. So as a family we've always spoken English together. My father taught me Greek but he would never allow my mother to speak it with me — he said she would ruin my grammar, but that would hardly matter as no one would understand my accent anyway!"

Alix laughed. "Your father sounds nice."

"I think he is. They both are." He glanced sideways at her. "You see, I have all the Cretan love of family. I would go to great lengths to prevent either of them being hurt in any way."

Again, that hint of a warning. Baffled and uneasy, Alix turned her head away and gazed out of the window. The countryside they were passing through was green and fertile, with a range of mountains running along the spine of the island. From a distance, the mountains looked bleak and grey, but already she knew that they were in fact smothered with tiny flowers, so that each was transformed into a giant rock garden. She smiled with pleasure as they passed two cherry trees in full blossom, with a view of distant, snow-capped mountains beyond — a view more likely to be attributed to Japan than Crete, she thought.

"This is the village of Ag Ioannis — Saint Joan," Lukas said. "There's a pleasant walk up that lane, on to the top of the hill. Wonderful views on all sides, and you can see both north and south coasts. Perhaps I'll take you up there one day."

"I shouldn't think so," Alix replied. "Not unless you think we might find Iphigenia on the summit."

Lukas said nothing and she felt a little ashamed of her rudeness. But it was essential to keep her purpose in mind — and hadn't he himself said that the sooner their search was over, the better he'd like it? The trouble was that the moment they started to relax and forget their antagonism towards each other, they both started to behave almost like friends.

Friends! she thought. That was the last thing she and Lukas could ever be. The word *lovers* came into her mind, and she pushed it away, then admitted that it was true. With an attraction between them that was almost visible, that vibrated in the air whenever they came too close, there was no doubt that she and Lukas could be lovers. The thought, coupled with the memory of their kisses, first in the doorway of his grandmother's home, then at the party last night, brought a shiver to her skin, yet at the same time it seemed as if she were melting inside.

Yes, she and Lukas could be lovers. But without friendship, without love, a purely sexual relationship would be empty and, in the end — for there would, inevitably, be an end — too painful. And Alix had had enough of pain.

The only answer was to keep him at a distance. Let him think her rude and unmannerly, if it was the only way. Accept his help in finding Iphigenia and then go her own way once more.

And when this is all over, she thought, and I'm back in London, I shall never, under any circumstances, go to the Minos again.

Their road took them along narrow, twisting ways, high on the hills and deep into olive groves. At times it was scarcely a road at all, little more than a track, with boulders and potholes that tossed the little car from side to side and made Alix fear for its survival. She looked at Lukas with accusing eyes, but he was concentrating on his driving and it was not until the surface suddenly improved to the state of an unmade road in England that she dared speak.

"Are you sure this is the way? There can't be

anywhere at the end of this!"

"Can't there?" He swung the car round the next corner and she saw to her surprise that they were running into a small village. The road was very nearly passable at this point, and old houses stood on either side, their walls cracked and stained, but obviously inhabited. At the end of the street she noticed some more imposing buildings, constructed with big slabs of stone. They had elaborately carved lintels and she gazed at them curiously.

"Old remains from the Roman or Minoan cultures," Lukas said briefly. "The island's full of them — most of them still used, never discovered by the archaeologists who make so much of Gortes and Knossos. You'll find people keeping chickens in old castles and using ancient walls as part of their farmyard."

"Or living in monasteries," Alix said, remembering his grandmother and reminded of something else that had puzzled her. Why did a family so clearly well off allow one of its oldest — and most respected, it seemed from the way they had treated her last night — members to live in such poor surroundings? She opened her mouth to ask Lukas, but before she could speak he had braked suddenly to avoid running into a donkey which had just ambled round the corner.

They continued out of the village and the road immediately worsened again. Alix remembered her doubts of a few moments ago and challenged him.

"Is it really necessary to use these rough tracks? Won't your aunt mind if you wreck her car? There must be better roads than this."

"Must there?" His brown eyes were still fixed on the road ahead, and she had to admit that it would have been foolhardy for him to have taken them off it for one second. "There's a law, is there, that says that Alix Berringer must always travel on smooth roads? Perhaps you think we should have reorganised the whole of Crete for your convenience."

She flushed. "Of course not. But —"

"This is what roads are like here," he stated. "This is a poor island. The main roads are, on the whole, very good. But there's too little money to spend it on roads between tiny villages." He spared her a scathing glance and she flinched. "You're accustomed to a country where money is spent like water on making everyone comfortable. It's not like that here."

Alix bit her lip. It was perfectly true, she thought, that most people in these tiny villages did seem to live very simply. Tiny stone cottages, donkeys for transport, old women leading goats and sheep to pasture and coming home with bundles of grass on their backs. It was all picturesque for the tourist, but what was its reality?

"It has its compensations," Lukas remarked, evidently following his own train of thought but seeming, for a moment, as if he were reading her mind. "They don't have to pack like sardines into a commuter train or risk being mugged in a city street. And it's quite a lot warmer than London!"

Alix relaxed and smiled, then felt the warmth spread through her body and immediately stiffened again. Wasn't this just what she had made up her mind to guard against?

It was some time later, when they had jolted their way through several more villages and Alix was beginning to wonder if they would ever reach their destination — if, indeed, they *had* a destination — that Lukas pulled up outside a tiny church and stopped the car. He looked around and smiled with satisfaction.

Alix gazed at their surroundings. The village was below them in a green, fertile bowl. Above, the hills rose on all sides, their flanks clothed in thick foliage. She could see vines neatly planted in rows, the silvery green of olive trees, and houses with a riot of flowers tumbling over white balconies.

There was no sound but that of birds singing, and the whisper of a breeze through the silver leaves.

"Is this it?" she asked, and her voice was hushed by the beauty of it. "Is this where Iphigenia lives?"

If it were, she thought, she must surely be happy, and her heart lifted at the thought of describing this place to her grandfather.

Lukas turned his head and looked at her. His eyes were dark, their expression unreadable. For a moment, he hesitated. Then he said in a light, almost careful tone, "This is where our search begins."

Slowly, as if unable to help himself, he lifted one hand and touched her face with his fingertips. Alix sat quite still, her blood storming through her veins. Her eyes locked with his.

His face changed slightly, as if the quality of the light had altered. Something flickered deep in his eyes. It was almost, she thought, a kind of regret.

But what could Lukas have to regret? That he had brought her here? That she was, in spite of his efforts, about to find Iphigenia?

Or was it something else entirely?

Chapter Eight

Lukas unfolded himself from the car and stood up, stretching his arms to the sky.

"Do you want to see inside the church?" he enquired as Alix got out on her side and stood looking about her. "It's small, but they're usually well looked after in these villages."

Alix glanced at him across the top of the car. His red shirt was open at the neck, revealing a tangle of curling black hair. He looked relaxed, content and very much a part of this landscape; as if he would be as much at home tending the olives or vines as running his restaurant in London.

"I think we ought to do what we came to do," she said hesitantly. "I don't have too much time really." But there was something about this dreaming valley that scorned the concept of time. As if here it had been stretched, so that although there was more of it, it must be used more slowly, as if to make haste would be a violation of the peace.

She looked at the little church. The heat shimmered about its white walls. Its tower was short but slender, in keeping with the delicacy of its structure. A bell hung at the top, its rope slung down and fastened to the door.

Lukas came round the car and moved past her to open the gate.

"I never feel I've visited a place unless I've been into its church," he declared. "It can't take long — it's not St Paul's Cathedral. And if you're going to be involved with Crete, you need to appreciate its culture."

He went into the little yard and put his hand on the door. The bell swung slightly, and he smiled and untied the rope, letting it swing free. "No point in letting the whole village know we've arrived until we're ready for them — though I dare say someone's already noticed us."

Alix looked back with some doubt. There was no sign of anyone in the valley and the village street was hidden from here. In fact, she wondered if there was anyone here at all. Perhaps they all worked in Rethymnon during the day.

She followed Lukas into the church and was immediately thankful that she had done so. Cool and dim, it took her a moment or two to adjust her sight, but as she did so the colours began to glow and she saw that the walls were covered with murals, a riot of blue and red and purple that depicted Christ in all the stages of his life, from the manger to the cross. The figures of the apostles were full of vigour — fishermen, brawny as any Cretan, hauling in their nets, a physician at his desk, a rent-collector taking in his dues. They looked real enough to have been painted from life, she thought, and perhaps they had been — from people the artist knew well, perhaps locals in this very village.

"It's beautiful," she said softly. "And so well kept. It seems . . . *cherished*."

Lukas was standing close to her shoulder. She could feel his warmth, but the tension between them was for the moment absent. He was gazing with absorption at the murals and at the carved wooden screen that sheltered the altar.

"I think all these churches are cherished," he said quietly. "Even the simplest. When we're back in Plakias I'll take you for a walk up the valley. There's an old mill there and a tiny church hollowed out of the rock. There's nothing there at all — no murals, no screen, only a rough wooden table for an altar. But it's used, it has its bottles of wine and oil, and its candles. And its own quiet atmosphere, just as the more elaborate churches have — perhaps all the more so for its simplicity."

This time, Alix made no curt, sarcastic rejoinder to his suggestion that they should go for a walk together. This was not the place for such ungraciousness. And the peace of the valley and the church, together with Lukas's air of contentment and obvious pleasure in the tiny church, had come together in a sense of homecoming which she was reluctant to destroy. A serenity she had not known for months.

She went to the door of the church and looked out, thinking of Rick. It was the first time his name had come into her mind without a stab of pain, pain composed partly of rejection, partly of humiliation at the way in which he had chosen to reject her. And that, she realised was all. There was no longer — if there had ever really been — the pain of having lost someone she truly loved.

Had she loved Rick? Or had it all been no more than an illusion?

She gazed down into the valley and the valley smiled back at her. You should know, it seemed to say. Just trust yourself to know real love when it comes to you.

Lukas was at her shoulder again and she turned and smiled up at him.

"Thank you. I'm glad we came into the church. And now . . . ?"

"Now you want to find Iphigenia." Again she surprised a flicker of something in his eyes and wondered if it could possibly be disappointment. And then it was gone, and their expression was veiled once more.

"Very well," he said. "Let's begin."

They left the car where it was and walked down the hill into the village. It was a tiny place — if Iphigenia was here, Alix thought, she must surely be easy to find — and although there was no actual taverna there was a small square with a spreading olive tree under which a few old men were sitting playing cards at a rickety table.

They glanced up as Alix and Lukas approached, watching them with eyes as black as olives set in their wrinkled faces. Each wore the traditional Cretan dress of black shirt, baggy breeches and high boots, with a black hat or scarf bound around the forehead. They looked at Lukas with no sign of recognition but greeted him and Alix courteously.

Lukas spoke to them in Greek for a few minutes, exchanging pleasantries, and introducing Alix — so that's another village given the idea that we're engaged, she thought with resignation — and within a few minutes extra chairs had been found from somewhere, two small glasses produced and they were being toasted with the fiery aniseed flavour of ouzo.

Alix sat silent, her face aching with the effort of smiling at people with whom she could not converse. There was an animated discussion going on now between Lukas and the old men, with much waving of hands. From the looks on their faces, they could have been discussing anything from the state of the world to the latest football results. Suddenly they all broke into roars of laughter and leaned back, slapping their thighs, and she felt the annoyance that always comes from watching other people laugh at a joke one cannot understand.

Lukas turned to her, his face alight with merriment, and started to explain, but she cut in sharply.

"It won't sound nearly so funny to me. Why don't you just get on and ask them about Iphigenia?"

He stopped abruptly, the laughter fading from

his face, and she felt as guilty as if she had slapped a child. His smile had transformed him, turning him from a remote stranger to a likeable, engaging — what a word *that* was to come to mind! — companion, the sort of companion it would be fun to spend a holiday with. *This* sort of holiday, she thought, pottering around the tiny lanes and villages of a foreign country, with no grand sightseeing tour, just a relaxed, unhurried exploration with time to sit under olive trees and set the world to rights with whoever happened along . . .

But this wasn't a holiday, she reminded herself, and if it were Lukas would be the last person she'd be spending it with. She hardened her heart against his wounded expression — it was probably assumed, anyway, for hadn't he proved himself an expert liar? — and repeated, "When are you going to ask them if she's here?"

Lukas spoke in a clipped voice. "It would hardly be polite to come rushing up to them like a couple of cheque-book journalists — naturally though that might come to you — demanding information about one of their own neighbours. One of them might even be her husband, had that occurred to you? It's necessary, and polite, to spend a little time talking to them first. Otherwise they're likely to just clam up. And you wouldn't want that, would you?"

Alix bit her lip. She was aware that she had just crushed something beautiful and precious. The peace of the valley, of the morning itself, had disappeared in one flash of her unruly tongue. It was like stepping on a butterfly.

"I'm sorry," she said quietly, and because the men were watching in some bewilderment she put out her hand and laid it upon his.

There was an immediate sense of relaxation in the little group. But Alix did not look at them. She was gazing at Lukas, her eyes locked with his, unable to turn away. She saw his pupils dilate and caught her breath.

He spoke again, and the curtness had gone, leaving his voice husky.

"Do you have the sketch? I'll show it to them now."

Wordlessly, Alix produced it from her bag and he laid it on the table and asked the men a question.

They leaned over it, their wrinkled faces intent, black eyes narrowed. To some of them it was upside down and one reached out and swivelled it round in order to examine it more closely. For several minutes they gazed at it, murmuring to each other, while Alix watched tensely. Then, to her dismay, they shook their heads and handed the sketch back.

Lukas took it and gave it a long look before returning it to her. His face was unreadable, his eyes hooded.

"I'm sorry, Alix. They don't recognise her at all."

Alix gazed at him. Her disappointment was equalled only by a sense that this was what he had expected. And yet he had sounded almost regretful. Why? He'd stated quite unequivocally that he didn't want her to find Iphigenia. Why should it matter to him that she hadn't, after all, lived in this village?

Alix took the sketch and looked at it herself before putting it back in her bag. Sadness filled her eyes with tears and the lovely young face swam before her. Such love, she thought, such eagerness, and all lost. And unless I can find her, she'll never know how her lover yearned for her, how he thinks of her still. And he'll never know what happened to her.

So long ago. How old had she been when he had made this sketch? Eighteen, twenty? What chance was there of recognising this young beauty in the aged wrinkles of the woman she would be now?

A sudden thought struck her and she looked up at Lukas with renewed hope.

"How old was Iphigenia when she moved away from Sellia?"

The question seemed to startle him. He frowned and looked nonplussed.

"I don't know — thirty, perhaps forty. I don't think anyone said."

"Why not?" But without waiting for an answer, she rushed on. "If she was thirty or forty years old when she moved, she wouldn't have looked like this any more. You're asking them to remember a young girl, and they probably never knew her like this. Ask if any older women moved into the village say, thirty or forty years ago."

Put like that, it seemed unlikely that anyone would remember. Thirty or forty years were a long time, and from the look Lukas gave her he evidently thought so too. But in such a tiny village as this, there could not have been many newcomers and surely it would always be remembered that a certain person had not grown up there as a child. She gazed appealingly at him and, after a moment, he turned back to put a question to the old men.

They listened, asked one or two questions of their own, then shrugged. Obviously they knew nothing of any such incomer. It seemed that the search had reached a dead end.

Lukas was chatting again, relaxed and easy on his little chair, and Alix sat quiet, fighting down her disappointment. What had she expected, after all? That they would leap upon the sketch with cries of recognition and lead her straight to the house where Iphigenia lived? It was fifty years since she had looked like that. She probably wouldn't even recognise herself! For the first time, the mission seemed impossible and Alix faced the bleak thought of failure.

I can't give up, she told herself. Not so soon. This is only the second day. But where else do I look?

After a few more minutes it became evident that Lukas was wishing the old men goodbye. There was much shaking of hands and well-wishing, a last glass of ouzo was proffered — and smilingly refused — and then she found herself walking back along the narrow street. Two old women sitting in a doorway, making lace, greeted them as they passed and Alix looked into their faces, trying desperately to find some resemblance to Iphigenia, but there was none. And again she thought, but there wouldn't be. I could pass her a hundred times and never know it.

Back at the car, she paused and looked hopelessly at Lukas.

"What now? I suppose you'll tell me there's no point in searching any further and take me back to Plakias?"

To her surprise, he shook his head.

"By no means. We've hardly begun. This isn't the only small village in this area. There are dozens of them tucked away in the hills."

Alix stared at him. "You mean it could be any one of a number? I thought you said it was this particular one."

"No, only that it was a small village in this part of the Rethymnon region." He grinned. "A nice excuse to go sightseeing in some of the more remote villages. Have you noticed we haven't seen a single tourist all morning?"

Alix brushed this aside. "But if there are so many, it could take weeks! And do we have to drink ouzo at every one?"

He burst out laughing and she thought once again how laughter transformed his face. He was no longer stern and forbidding, the dominant male, but young and friendly, the humour sparkling in his eyes. He shook his head at her again.

"Oh, Alix, you'll be the death of me. A short-cut to alcoholism! No, we won't have to drink ouzo every time we stop, though we might have difficulty in refusing, the Cretans are so hospitable and can be very hurt if their hospitality is rejected. But for every glass of ouzo we're offered, we'll probably get a cup of coffee next time. Do you think you can stand it?"

She smiled back a little reluctantly, unable to maintain her own frostiness. "I'll do my best. So — do we go on to the next place now?"

"No." He reached into the car and pulled out the map. "What we do now is look for a pleasant spot to have lunch. I thought we'd go on down the valley — there's another village further down, see, and there's a bridge over the river shortly before you reach it. We'll stop there."

They got into the car. Once again, Alix was conscious of Lukas's nearness and warmth. He started the engine and as he took off the handbrake his fingers brushed her thigh. She felt the tingle instantly, running down to her toes and up into her abdomen where it seemed to curl itself into a tight, shivering knot. She turned and looked at him, and he removed his hand as if he had been stung.

The stream was in the bottom of the valley, tumbling down through the woods in a series of tinkling waterfalls. Lukas parked the car in a shady spot and opened the boot, removing Alix's rucksack and his own, much larger, one.

"Let's walk upstream a bit, away from the road."

It was hardly a busy road, Alix thought, but she nodded and they set off along a narrow cobbled track between stone walls. Small, gnarled trees grew on either side, and the banks running down to the stream were grassy and sprinkled with wild flowers. One or two were quite startling — a huge purple spike in a hood of deep burgundy, like a giant arum lily and, in contrast, a patch of tiny white cyclamen like a patch of forgotten snow. Alix gazed about her, enraptured by the tranquil beauty, and when Lukas paused at last to suggest stopping, she could only nod her head speechlessly.

They had walked through the wood to a little clearing, dappled with sunlight. The grass here had been cropped short, probably by goats or sheep, but had been allowed to grow again so that it formed a soft turf. The bank formed a small plateau under a tumble of rocks, and the stream plunged over the ledge in a shimmering cascade.

They dropped their rucksacks on the ground and sat down. Alix drew up her knees and folded her arms about them, fascinated as always by the sight of water tumbling endlessly, each little drop taking its own individual course, each blending with the rest to make a shape that looked perpetually the same, until you looked closely and caught the million minute changes that happened every second. The curve above the fall was almost sensuous in its smoothness, shattering like glass as it fell into the pool beneath, breaking up the cool, dark surface and sending bright bubbles racing downstream.

Lukas unfastened his rucksack. "Did you bring any food?"

"Oh, yes." She jerked her attention away from the water and unbuckled the straps of her own bag. "Some cheese and fruit."

"Good. That'll go nicely with what I've got." To her astonishment, he drew out a small bottle of wine, wrapped in a padded cool bag. He took it out of the bag and placed it in the stream, wedged between two rocks. He then produced two wine glasses which he laid on the grass, and a box which he opened to reveal two cold joints of chicken, some salad and four fresh rolls.

"Good heavens," she said weakly, "is this your idea of a picnic?"

"It's simple enough," he said. "With your cheese and fruit — if there's enough to share — we shall have a very pleasant meal. Oh, and I've got a flask of hot water too, to make some coffee."

He handed Alix a plate and a paper napkin, and she helped herself to a piece of chicken and some salad. He had brought butter for the rolls, kept firm in the bottom of the coolbag, and cutlery. He doesn't miss a trick, she thought, half sourly, half in admiration.

Apart from the ripple of the water and the birdsong in the trees above, there was nothing to be heard. No engine noise, no tractor working in a distant field, no roar of jet planes streaming overhead, such as so often spoilt the peace of the English countryside. Alix and Lukas sat in silence, eating their lunch, each watching the water and the trees and busy with their thoughts.

At least, Alix supposed that Lukas was busy. When she stole a glance at him, he seemed almost to be half asleep, deep in meditation as he ate the food they had brought. Yet at the same time, he gave the impression of being totally absorbed both in what he was doing and what was going on around him. It was as if he had given himself up entirely to his surroundings, had merged into the environment and become part of it. With a tiny shock, she realized that this was the kind of concentration he would bring to everything he did — wholehearted participation, with nothing held back.

Before she could stop herself, she was imagining him bringing that kind of total commitment to the act of making love. The picture conjured up was almost frightening; the thought of looking up into that dark face, of being completely at his mercy, an awesome one. He would demand nothing less than total commitment from the woman he loved, she thought, and a shudder ran over her body.

Instantly, he was aware of it.

"Cold?" He glanced up at the sun beating

down from a hard blue sky. "I chose this spot partly for the shade. It's not good to sit out in the midday sun."

Mad dogs and Englishmen, she thought, stifling a bubble of hysterical laughter. "No, I'm not cold. Just — one of those shivers, you know."

He nodded, but his eyes rested upon her face as if he were trying to read her mind. She thought of the previous occasions when he had seemed to do just that, and of the way he seemed to know so much about her and why she was in Crete. Who are you? she thought. A London restaurateur, half Cretan, half Scottish, but what else? What does such a combination produce?

"Let's have some wine," he said, reaching for the bottle that was still in the stream. He uncorked it and poured some into each glass. It was a delicate straw-yellow, and when Alix lifted it to her lips the scent was flowery yet with a tang of sharpness. She sipped it and let the ice-cold liquid trickle over her tongue and down her throat.

"It's delicious."

"My aunt makes it herself. You won't find it served in the restaurant though — not unless you're a very special customer." He smiled at her. "Which you now are, of course."

Alix dropped her eyes, studying the glass between her fingers. It was cut-glass, its facets sparkling in the sunlight, sending out tiny flashes of rainbow light. She sipped again and looked up to find Lukas still watching her.

"What — what are you looking at?" she asked in a voice which was unexpectedly creaky.

"I'm looking at you." His voice was suddenly soft, almost caressing. He reached over, slowly and without hurry, taking the half-empty glass from her fingers. Carefully, he set it down on a rock, and then moved closer and drew her into his arms.

Alix's heart leapt and began to beat rapidly. She made an effort to speak but her voice seemed to have failed completely. She licked her lips to try again and saw Lukas's eyes follow the movement. His hand was stroking her hair, his fingers touching the skin of her neck. They slid round to the back of her head and held it while he laid his lips on hers.

"Lukas . . ." But her words were lost in the roaring of blood in her ears, in the fire that his touch had kindled in her body. She could feel the radiance of his warmth searing her veins and the touch of his fingertips was like the flicker of flames running across her skin. His hand slipped down her back, tracing her spine so that she arched against him, and he dropped his lips to the hollow of her throat and held her close, her breasts crushed against the hardness of his chest.

He was muttering something she could not hear. His mouth was buried now in the cleft between her breasts, his teeth teasing open the buttons of her shirt. Alix's head dropped back, weakness invading her so that she had no power to resist, even if she had wanted to. And she didn't want to. She wanted his kissing to go on, she wanted his caresses to take her further, higher, until she was swinging amongst the stars. She wanted him to love her — fully, completely, totally . . .

Totally! The word struck her like a hammer. What had she been thinking, only a few moments ago — that Lukas would bring to his lovemaking a wholehearted commitment, holding nothing back. And that he would expect such total giving also on the part of his partner.

With a gasp of dismay, she twisted in his arms, wriggling free. At first, he took her movements for those of pleasure and tightened his arms about her, and she was afraid that he had gone too far to stop. But a moment later he seemed to realise that she was resisting him, and instantly loosened his grip, though he kept his arms lightly about her body.

"What is it?" His dark eyes searched her face. "Alix, what's the matter?"

"I — I can't." She sought for an explanation, knowing she could not tell him her thoughts about commitment and her fear of giving herself with such abandon. Instead, she remembered the antagonism there had been between them, her determination to keep that antagonism alive to maintain the distance between them. What had happened to that resolve? Had a picnic beside a waterfall and half a glass of wine been enough to crumble it?

"I won't make love to you," she went on more

strongly. "Just because we're alone in a romantic place, it doesn't mean that I'm ready for a little dalliance. I'm not in the market for that kind of thing."

"That's not the impression you gave me," he drawled, and her face burned. "You seemed quite as ready as I was."

His eyes were hooded again and she felt a flash of annoyance. Why couldn't he reveal his feelings? Why did he have to hide all the time? She looked at him steadily and was rewarded by a flicker of emotion deep inside.

"Yes," she said, taking a deep breath, "I have to admit that there's an attraction between us. A purely physical attraction that means nothing, and that I wish wasn't there. And which I am doing my *best* to resist. I just wish you would try as well."

"And do you think I don't?" he demanded with sudden fire. "Do you think I *want* to get myself involved with someone who . . . who —"

"Who what?" Alix challenged. "Go on, Lukas. Say what you were going to say. Who *what?*"

He hesitated, then relaxed suddenly, so that the taut lines of his face and body softened. His eyes were once more liquid, almost tender as they gazed at her, and she felt a quiver of emotion that was more than physical, stir within her.

"Never mind," she said quickly. "I know just what you really think of me. And you must have a pretty good idea what I think of you, too. So as you said this morning, why don't we get this business over, and we'll both be free to go our own ways?"

"You mean you want to go on with your search," he said flatly. "You're not interested in anything else."

She opened her eyes at him. "Of course I want to go on with it. That's why I'm here. And no — I'm not interested in anything else. Nor any*one* else."

He gave her a long look. For a baffling moment she had the impression of sadness, and when he spoke his voice was soft.

"Oh Alix, Alix," he said, and moved a little closer, his brown eyes searching hers. "What have you got yourself mixed up in?"

"Mixed up in?" She backed away. "I don't know what you mean."

"This search," he said. "Why is it so important to you? What will be your reward if you succeed?"

Alix stared at him. "But you already know. You've made it clear that you know. How or why, I have no idea — but you do, don't you?"

"I thought I did," he said, and again there was a touch of something very like sadness in his tone. "I'd begun to hope that I was wrong." He paused, then added, "Why don't you give it up? Abandon it now, before it's too late. This world isn't for you, Alix. Money, materialism, they wreck people's lives. And to exploit others for their sake —"

"I'm sorry," Alix cut in, "I don't know what

you're talking about. I've no intention of exploiting anyone. I simply want to find an old woman, for reasons that are nothing to do with you. It has nothing to do with materialism or money. And I have no, repeat *no*, intention of abandoning my search now." She gave him a defiant look. "With or without your help."

He returned her gaze and said quietly, "And I suppose you mean to hold me to the bargain we made."

Alix shrugged. "That's entirely up to you. It doesn't matter to me that you'll be made to look both foolish and a liar before your whole family. It's no more than the truth, after all." But there was a pang in her heart nonetheless as she thought of all the people who had wished her well last night, of the welcome they had given her into their family and, most of all, of the delight on the face of the old grandmother.

And there was another pang too, for the other Lukas of whom she had caught such revealing glimpses. The man with an appreciation of beauty, a love of family life, a humour that lit up his entire face and a tenderness that showed when he slipped his arm around her to keep her warm.

There was no tenderness in his face now, no humour dancing in his eyes. Instead, he could have been carved from stone as he turned away from her and began to pack up the remains of the picnic. He stood up and looked around to see that nothing had been left behind.

180

"Then we'd better go," he said tersely. "I was going to suggest we walk into the village from here — it's a little longer, by the cobbled path, but more attractive than the road. But I won't ask you to waste your time."

He set off, striding along the track as if he had a train to catch. And Alix, feeling once again that she had stepped on something precious, lifted her rucksack on to her back and followed him.

Chapter Nine

Alix got back into the car, her heart heavy with disappointment and frustration. A wasted afternoon, she thought. And yet — if only she and Lukas could have been in accord, and not engaged in a search which divided them as much as it had brought them together — it could have been such fun.

The village had been quiet when they'd arrived, and at first she had thought it must be deserted. But a closer look at the houses, tumbling down their narrow, hilly streets, betrayed the slight movement of curtains and the occasional glimpse of a face, peering out.

"I suppose they don't get many visitors here," she remarked, pausing to admire a huge fall of rock roses that hung like a white cascade over a garden wall. "It's so peaceful. We might have stepped back a thousand years in time — except for the TV aerials!"

"Yes, you needn't worry about that — they're modern enough to watch TV," Lukas said, and she glanced at him, surprised by the bite in his tone. He was walking slightly ahead of her, almost as if he didn't want to acknowledge the fact that they were together. Suits me, she thought with a mental shrug, except that I don't much relish the idea of walking three steps behind, like a concubine. But with the difference in their height, there was no possibility of matching Lukas's long stride, and she refused to run along beside him as if she were a little dog being taken for a walk.

"Do they have a taverna here?" she asked, trying not to sound breathless.

Lukas glanced at her over his shoulder. Until now, he had not spoken to her since they had left the little picnic spot, and had barely looked at her. His face was still grim and her heart sank at the thought of spending more days like this, travelling to remote villages and conducting their search in hostile silence.

Wasn't it what you wanted? a small voice asked. But her heart yearned for the Lukas who had revealed himself at the party, leaping and spinning in the dance, letting his rich baritone voice flood the room with throbbing sound, the Lukas who had bent to kiss his grandmother's cheek, a look of ineffable tenderness on his face. Who had slipped his arm about her shoulders to keep her warm. And the Lukas who had covered her lips with his and drawn from her a response that left her quivering, and longing for more.

"A taverns?" he said, and his voice was cold. "I've no idea. I don't know these villages at all. I dare say there's some place where the men meet to drink together and discuss the day's events, but it may not be your idea of a taverna."

"Oh, and just what *is* my idea of a taverna?" she asked, irritated by his barbed remarks. Couldn't he at least be polite? "Do tell me. I'm fascinated to know."

Lukas looked annoyed and for a moment she thought he wasn't going to answer. Then he said tersely, "Don't push me too far, Alix. We both know what you're looking for — somewhere picturesque, with plenty of flowers to give colour and everyone in their best national dress celebrating at a party and smashing plates left, right and centre!"

Alix stared at him, taken aback by the cutting sarcasm of his tone. What on earth was he talking about — and why did he sound so resentful? With an attempt at lightness, she said, "Well, we had all that last night and very nice it was too."

"I know," he said bitterly. "When I think how we played right into your hands —"

This was too much. Alix reached out a hand and grabbed his arm, forcing him to stop and turn to her. She planted her feet squarely on the concrete road and faced him.

"Look, Lukas," she said, giving each word its own emphasis, "I don't know what you mean by that and I'm not sure I care. But you might remember that last night's party wasn't *my* idea — in fact, if I'd had any inkling it was going to happen, I'd have steered well clear. Nor was our pseudo engagement my idea — that was your brilliant way of getting out of an awkward situation. A situation that was only awkward for *you*, I might add! In fact, if it hadn't been for that one lie which you decided you had to tell, to save your face with your grandmother, none of this whole sham would have had to happen and I'd have found someone else to help me find Iphigenia."

"Like your friend with the yellow hair and car salesman smile, I suppose," Lukas said nastily.

"Yes, very likely," Alix replied calmly. "Why not? He seems the obvious person to ask."

"I'm amazed you didn't arrange it that way from the beginning," he said. "Or perhaps you did and then cottoned on to me as someone who knew the area and the people and might do the job quicker."

"For the last time," Alix said, starting to lose her temper, "I did *not* 'cotton on' to you. This whole situation is one of your engineering. And I don't know why we're standing here in the road arguing about it —"

"D'you know a better place?"

"— when all I asked was if there was a taverna here."

"And all *I* said was —"

Their voices were rising. Suddenly embarrassingly aware of it, Alix looked round and saw a small boy standing at the edge of the road, his dark eyes fixed on them. Abruptly, she stopped shouting and threw Lukas a look of entreaty.

"Please," she said in a low voice, "don't let's spoil this place by quarrelling."

His eyes and face had been angry, but at her words he subsided. He too glanced at the boy, who looked from one to the other and then spoke.

"Come," he said, gesturing with a grubby hand. "You come."

Alix looked at Lukas. "What does he want?"

"Come," the boy said again, and turned as if to walk away. He looked over his shoulder. "You come."

Lukas grinned suddenly, his face relaxing so that once again he looked young and carefree. "He wants us to go with him."

Alix had worked that out for herself, but she didn't say so. There was no point in starting another argument, and she didn't want that hostile expression back on his face, hardening its strong lines. She much preferred Lukas in his relaxed mode.

The boy, evidently satisfied now that they were following him, set off along a narrow lane, leading between the houses. Alix glanced about her with interest, noticing several more old walls of the type that Lukas had told her were signs of ancient Roman or Minoan civilizations. What archaeological riches there must be in these villages, she thought. And there must be even more than could be seen at a quick glance, like this — mosaic pavements hidden under the concrete roads, perhaps, or in the tumbledown houses.

They came to the edge of the village. Above them, on a shelf in the hillside, they could see a

186

larger house, overlooking the roofs. A wide, twisting path led up to it.

"He's taking us to his home," Alix murmured.

The boy stopped. His face was full of pride as he indicated a small construction at the side of the road. It consisted of an amphora and a tank, with pipes and tubes leading from one to the other. Alix stared at it, nonplussed, and Lukas laughed.

"It's a still! His father evidently makes his own liquor."

"A *still?* But — is that allowed?"

"Oh yes. You see quite a few of them scattered around the villages. It would be considered a serious infringement of liberty not to be allowed to distil one's own ouzo. After all, they make their own wine — what's the difference?"

Alix shook her head, unable for the moment to think of a difference. But there was no time to discuss it. The boy was off again, leading them up the track. He pointed to some hens scratching in the dust.

"Chickens." A dog emerged from a kennel and leapt on the end of its chain. "Dog." He said something else, a word Alix did not catch but which was evidently the dog's name. Before she could ask him to repeat it, he scampered on, leading them up a flight of steps to a terrace in front of the house.

"Oh!" Alix said, pausing at the top. "Oh, how lovely."

The terrace was built into the corner of an

L-shape, roofed over with glass which was almost obscured by the plants which scrambled over it on both sides. Vines, wisteria, clematis, all vied together for space and produced a tangle of colour and foliage. Around the sides of the terrace was an array of pots and amphorae, all thick with flowers. The clear red of geraniums, the brilliant orange splashes of nasturtiums and the pinks and mauves of impatiens blended together to make the terrace a garden of almost aching brightness.

At one side, a door led into the house, and as they came up the steps a young woman emerged, followed by a tumble of small children.

"Hello." She smiled at them, clearly shy but also excited to be welcoming them to her home. "Come. Sit." She indicated a daybed and some chairs. "You drink coffee?"

Alix glanced at Lukas. She was still not accustomed to the Cretan way of inviting passers-by into their homes and plying them with refreshments. But he smiled back reassuringly, all his earlier antagonism set aside and spoke to the woman in Greek.

Her face lit up and she laughed, obviously both surprised and pleased to find him speaking her language. Immediately, they were immersed in a rapid conversation, followed with interest by the small boy who had led Alix and Lukas here.

Alix felt a touch on her knee and looked down to see a tiny girl, aged about two, gazing up into her face. The child said something and Alix smiled. It was hopeless enough trying to communicate with adults, there was no possibility at all of understanding a two-year-old! But the toddler seemed accustomed to being misunderstood and had other methods to employ. She dragged at Alix's hands and tried to scramble up on to her knee.

"Oh, if that's what you want!" Alix said, and lifted her up. The little girl snuggled into her body and Alix settled her arms around her and smiled at the ring of faces which had gathered about to stare.

There were three other children, two boys and an older girl. All looked younger than the first boy, who Alix guessed to be about ten. The girl was probably eight or nine, the boys two and four years younger. A nicely spaced family, Alix thought, and smiled at them, nodding at their chatter.

The older of the two boys broke away from the ring and ran over to a cage that stood in the corner. He reached in his hand and pulled out a bundle of feathers which he brought across to show her.

"It's a baby bird," she said, forgetting that they did not understand. "It looks like a greenfinch." Gently, she stroked the yellow and green feathers. "Oh, it's so tiny — where did you find it?"

A chorus of information met her query, and the children began to grab with fierce little hands for the privilege of holding the bird. Alix held it up out of their reach but they took this for a game and began leaping to snatch at her hand. In a few seconds the older boy, his face alight with mischief, had regained possession of the tiny creature and began tossing it in the air.

"Oh — no!" Alix exclaimed in distress, but he only laughed, ran to the other end of the terrace and threw it to his brother. They began a game of catch, the little bird cheeping and fluttering tiny wings in an effort to stay in the air.

"Lukas," she said, catching at his hand. "Stop them — they're hurting the poor little thing."

Lukas turned away from his conversation and saw what was happening. The nestling had dropped to the ground now and the toddler seized her chance and scrambled down from Alix's lap to clutch it. She held it close against her chest, obviously determined not to let it go, and Lukas prised open her small fingers.

"Ochi, ochi," he said softly, shaking his head. "Too small. Too small." With infinite gentleness he took the baby bird and examined its tiny body. Then, shaking his head again at the clamour from the children who were leaping about him, trying to snatch it away, he carried it over to the cage and put it back inside. He closed the door and spoke to the children in Greek.

"I doubt if they'll take a scrap of notice," he remarked, sitting down again beside Alix. "But at least the poor creature will get a few moments' respite."

"What did you tell them?"

"What do you think? That birds have feelings just like us, that we must do our best to be kind to them and not hurt them, that it was only a baby, that it would die unless they treated it well . . . All the things one would tell a child. But the attitude to such things is different here. They may remember, but my guess is that they'll have it out again the moment we walk away, and the poor little scrap will be dead by nightfall."

The woman had gone inside to make coffee and the toddler, denied her toy, began to cry. Alix lifted her on to her knee again, talking soothingly into her ear. She cuddled the little body against her. They didn't mean to be cruel, she knew. As Lukas said, the attitude was different. One could not censure them for it.

The child stopped crying and snuggled against her. Alix stroked the tangled hair. She felt the warmth of the little body and cradled it in her arms. Then she looked up and met Lukas's eyes.

He was gazing at her with an expression she had never seen before. A look almost of wonder. Of tenderness. And of some powerful emotion, as if somewhere inside he had been given a revelation.

Alix felt a movement deep within her body. She caught her breath, and stared at him, unable to turn her eyes away. And then the woman came out of her kitchen, bearing a tray filled with cups and glasses, and the moment was gone.

It did not come again. The gathering rapidly developed into a party, with several of the neighbours dropping in and much talk and laughter. A few could speak a little English, but it was soon exhausted and the chatter became exclusively Greek. Once again, Alix found herself listening with a fixed smile on her face, but they did their best to include her and Lukas translated from time to time. But his moment of emotion seemed to have passed and his voice was cool again, leaving her in no doubt that they were still as far apart as ever.

She sighed and gazed out from the terrace, over the little village. The children had grown bored and skipped away to play in the little wood behind the garden. Even the toddler had slipped off her knee and gone down the steps to make mud pies. The men were now discussing something, their voices earnest, and the women had disappeared into the house. Alix wished she could speak Greek, so that she could talk to them, find out what life was like for a woman in these remote villages.

There was a slight lull in the conversation and she said to Lukas, "You might remember why we're here. Have you asked them about Iphigenia yet?"

"Not yet. It's necessary —"

"I know. To be polite. To let them feel at ease." She hated the note of sarcasm in her voice but seemed unable to keep it out. "But at this rate it's going to take forever."

He glanced at her, his eyes hooded. "I imagine that's quite possible."

Alix stared at him. She said slowly, "You're not really trying to find Iphigenia at all, are you? Why should you? You never wanted me to in the first place, and —"

Lukas cut in sharply. "Don't start another scene here, Alix. These people don't deserve it. I'll ask them as soon as the moment's right." He turned back to the men and said something which made them all roar with laughter.

At her, presumably. Alix felt her face flame and sat saying nothing, staring out again at the wooded valley. Below the house was a neat vegetable plot and a small vineyard. An old woman hobbled out of one of the cottages and bent over something in her garden.

Could she be Iphigenia?

A sound made her turn and she saw that the men were shifting their chairs. Lukas had taken the sketch out of her rucksack and was showing it to them. They bent over it, staring intently, asking questions, tracing the lines of the young face with their fingers. There was a moment or two of discussion and then they shook their heads and handed the sheet of paper back.

Another fiasco.

She thought of Lukas's words. *Don't start another scene here, Alix.* Her face burned again — weren't they the words Rick had used, that last night in the Minos? But *he'd* started that scene. He'd waited until they were halfway through their main course to tell her that he was breaking their engagement. That the wedding was off.

He'd told her then because he knew how she hated scenes in public, because he thought her loathing of them would prevent her from showing her reaction. But how could anybody hear news like that and hold back their feelings?

Alix had been startled by her own reaction. She had never thought to find herself behaving so dramatically in public, in a place where she was known. The moment she saw the wine cascading over Rick's head, running down his astounded face, she had been overwhelmed by shame and humiliation, and had barely been able to see through her tears enough to stumble to the door. And it was there that she had found someone holding out her coat, ready for her to slip her arms into the sleeves. And she had looked up into dark eyes, eyes like brown silk, eyes that were soft and liquid with compassion . . .

Lukas. She could scarcely believe now that she had not known him immediately, that first moment as they waited to board the plane. For he had known her. He recalled, she knew, every moment of her humiliation on that terrible evening.

But she had tried to blot it from her mind, tried to blot out everything connected with it. She hadn't *wanted* to recognise him.

The pain was still there. But she knew now that it was still the memory of a past humiliation that hurt. It had nothing to do with lost love — clearly, the love she had thought Rick had for her had been no more than an illusion. And hers for him had been killed by his cruelty.

Rick had not been the man she thought him. And she realised that she need worry no longer about why he had left her, what it was in her that had caused his change of heart. It wasn't her problem, it was his.

The realisation brought a lift to her heart. But even that could not compensate for her disappointment over the afternoon — although she wasn't sure now just what she was most disappointed about. Was it because the search for Iphigenia had once more proved fruitless? Or because she and Lukas were once again distant from each other, their moments of rapport almost thrust away as if neither wanted to acknowledge them?

It had been easy, in the end, to detach themselves from the party. The women had emerged from the house with trays of food — chips and fried rabbit — and then there had been little honey cakes and *bougatsa* to follow. The wine had flowed freely — though Alix was relieved to see that Lukas drank very little — and then there was more coffee. And all the time, fresh people kept arriving, so that in the end she thought the entire village must be crowded on to the terrace. And although the gathering had formed in their honour, it finally became apparent that they were no longer needed, that the celebration would continue quite happily without them.

Unobtrusively, they said goodbye to their hostess and her husband who had, by this time, arrived home from the vineyard, and slipped away to the car.

"Well, that was quite a party," she said, trying to keep her voice light. She wasn't at all sure of Lukas's attitude towards her now. Was he still hostile or had he relaxed again? It had been impossible to tell for the past hour. But his clipped voice and the hard edge to his tone swiftly removed her doubts.

"Yes, I'm sorry you had to endure it. Perhaps next time we'll be luckier and find a village that won't insist on treating you like an honoured guest." He started the engine and revved it unnecessarily.

Alix caught her breath. "Do you have to be quite so unpleasant?"

"No," he said after a pause, "but it helps."

"Helps?" She stared at him but he kept his face firmly turned towards the road ahead. "What do you mean?"

Lukas sighed. Alix looked more closely at his face and saw that it was taut with emotion. But was it only anger that she saw there, in the hard lines of his jaw, the tightness about his eyes? He looks unhappy too, she thought, and felt a misery of her own welling up inside her.

"Why do we have to quarrel all the time?" she asked, and her voice sounded small and lonely. "Please, Lukas, can't we start again?"

"Back at my grandmother's house, you

mean?" He shook his head. "It wouldn't do any good."

"No, before that. Back at the taverna in Sellia. It was there, wasn't it — something happened there that set you against me." She touched his arm. "It's to do with my search for Iphigenia. That's what made you angry in the first place. But why?"

He sighed again. "If you really don't know, Alix —"

"But I don't! How can I? You say you know why I'm looking for her, but I don't see how you *can* know. I haven't discussed it with anyone —"

"Not even your boss?"

"My *boss*?" She stared at him. "But what's *he* got to do with it?" She thought of John Kitchener, giving her his blessing for this trip to Crete, telling her they didn't need her for the new section of the science magazine for another three weeks. Did he and Lukas know each other? Had he, for some reason she couldn't begin to fathom, talked to Lukas about her? "Lukas, please stop staring at the road and look at me!"

"If I stop staring at the road," he said tersely, "we shall crash. As you can see for yourself."

"Then stop the car." Alix was beginning to feel angry again. "Lukas, we've got to talk about this."

For a moment or two he did not answer. Then he swung the car off the rough track and on to a grassy patch under a large olive tree. He stopped the engine.

"Go on, then. Talk."

Alix gazed at him. His face was like stone. He did not look at her, but stared ahead through the windscreen.

She felt helpless. It was like trying to enlist the sympathy of a statue. And her helplessness brought a fresh anger. He was doing it deliberately, she knew. Shutting himself away from her, not even giving her the *chance* to explain . . .

"Are you sure you know why I'm looking for Iphigenia?" she asked quietly. "You keep saying you know, but it seems more and more to me that you must have the wrong idea. Why don't you tell me what you think my reason is?"

"Why don't *you* tell me your reason?" he countered swiftly.

Alix sighed. "Very well." She hesitated. "It all goes back a long way. You must know what happened here during the Second World War. Greece was occupied by the Germans but Crete refused to succumb and started the Battle of Crete to protect their island. Britain, Australia and New Zealand sent forces here to help protect them, but the Germans invaded and drove them out. Some of the soldiers escaped, others were caught and taken prisoner, and Crete was occupied like mainland Greece."

"I'm aware of all that," he said coldly. "It's my family history. Go on."

"Some of the soldiers were taken into Cretan homes, to be looked after and hidden," she said in a low voice. "Some of them fell in love. Iphigenia —"

"Right, that's enough," he broke in, and she realised with dismay that his voice was still as hard. "You've said enough for me to know that I was right. Iphigenia fell in love with one of these soldiers. He went away, promising to return for her once the war was over — and never came back. And now you've come to find her, to bring them together again."

"How do you know?"

He looked at her for the first time, a glance of such withering scorn she was surprised she didn't shrivel up on the spot.

"Like Romeo and Juliet, it's a common enough story. Your soldier wasn't the only one to take advantage of a —"

"He did not take advantage!"

"How can you be so sure? Were you there? Have you talked to Iphigenia?"

"You know perfectly well I haven't!" Alix flared. "Because you won't let me!" There was a moment of pure stunned silence. She saw the expression flash across his face and drew in her breath. "That's it, isn't it," she said quietly. "I had a suspicion earlier, now I'm sure I'm right. You're doing this deliberately. Taking me to villages where you're not known, where you can be sure Iphigenia isn't known. You're just pretending to help me — but what you're really doing is making certain I never come within ten miles of Iphigenia. Isn't that true? *Isn't it?*"

He turned again and she met his eyes. Their darkness was absolute, with not even the rim of shimmering bronze to brighten them. It was as if a light had gone out.

"I'm right, aren't I?" she said tonelessly, and he nodded.

"Yes. You're right. I don't want you to find Iphigenia. I don't like what you're doing nor why you're doing it. And I've no intention — I've never had any intention — of helping you."

The silence was heavy now, almost palpable. It was like a thick impenetrable wall between them. Alix felt misery settle inside her like a lump of lead. She felt the tears in her eyes and hardly knew what they were for. The afternoon was suddenly bleak and cold, the warmth of the sunlight chilled, its brightness dimmed.

"Another lie," she said at last, and he nodded.

"But not any more. I've had enough of lies, Alix. Lies to my family, my friends, yes, even lies to you." His mouth twisted a little as he looked at her. "Believe it or not, I'm not accustomed to lying and it doesn't come easily. I did it in the first place only to protect my grandmother. It grew and got out of hand. I had my reasons — good reasons, in my opinion — but now I've had enough." He waved his hand at the village they had just left. "It's spreading all over the island. All these good people, I'm lying to them as well. As you say, I've been choosing places where I'm sure Iphigenia has never set foot. Accepting their hospitality, taking up their time." He looked at her again. "You may be quite accustomed to this sort of thing, but I'm not. I feel sickened by it."

"*You* feel sickened by it?" She barely registered the rest of his words. "How do you think *I* feel?"

"Pretty annoyed, I should think, at the waste of your precious time. So we'll call it a day, shall we?" He started the engine again.

"Just a moment." Alix laid her hand on his arm. "If you're going back on our bargain, refusing to help me look for Iphigenia —"

"Oh, I am, believe me. There's no *if* about it."

"If you're doing that," she went on, ignoring his interruption, "what are you going to do about our engagement? Are you going to tell your family it's broken off? Because you can hardly hide the fact that we're not seeing each other any longer."

"I shan't even try. I told you, I'm tired of lies."

"So what are you going to tell them?" Alix persisted.

Lukas looked at her. The engine was running softly and he had his hand on the brake lever, as if ready for a quick start. There was a moment of tense silence and then he said quietly, "Why, the truth of course. What else is there to tell?"

"You mean, the story of Iphigenia — everything?"

"Everything."

"But that will make my position here quite untenable. I won't have a hope of finding her once you've given them your version. Nobody will help me!"

"Exactly," he said, and released the handbrake. "So wouldn't it be best if you got on the next plane back to England and left Crete for ever? And left us all in peace?"

Chapter Ten

The beach at Plakias was deserted that evening. The few holidaymakers had gone back to their hotels and apartments and the blue umbrellas had all been folded in case a wind sprang up over-night. The small, crinkling waves rippled lazily across the wide bay and broke in a lacy cream foam on the shingle. A boat chugged quietly into the harbour.

Alix wandered slowly along the edge of the water. It was clear and cold, and she could see the stones gleaming under the burnished path thrown down by the setting sun. As she had often done when a small child, she stood and gazed at the pathway, wondering what it would be like to walk along it, where such a mysterious road might lead. Anywhere, so long as it was away from Crete, she thought sadly. Anywhere away from Lukas.

What had been happening between them? She thought of the drive home, the silence that had hung like a heavy blanket in the car, smothering all possibility of communication. A silence composed of more than hostility, more than anger. There had been something else in it too, she thought, something that went even deeper.

Some strong emotion that neither had brought into the open.

She thought of the powerful attraction between them and remembered her earlier conviction, that she and Lukas could have been lovers. It had been there during their arguments too, the knowledge that if only this conflict over Iphigenia did not lie between them, there would have been nothing to prevent their coming together. Nothing to keep their bodies apart, nothing to separate their minds and their hearts.

Minds and hearts! But that's love, she thought blankly. Not simply physical desire, but love, love that runs deep and true. A love that is physically expressed, but which involves so much more than the body . . .

Was it possible that such a love could exist between herself and Lukas?

To her astonishment and consternation, Alix found her cheeks suddenly wet with tears. She rubbed at them with the backs of her hands, furious at their betrayal. She did *not* love Lukas! She'd only known him a day, for heaven's sake. How could anyone fall in love in the space of one day?

A day! Was that really all it was since she'd met him? No, it was longer than that. Two days — forty-eight hours since she'd first walked into his uncle's taverna. And before that, on the plane. And before *that,* in his restaurant in London.

Oh, big deal, she jeered at herself. Twice as long as you thought. Plenty of time to fall in love.

After all, it didn't take you long to think you hated him, did it?

But I don't know him well enough, she argued, and knew that was not true. She knew Lukas very well indeed.

She had seen the true Lukas when he had demanded that his grandmother must not be scandalised by their kiss in her doorway. She had seen the true Lukas when he had flung himself with such wholehearted enjoyment into the traditional dances, when he had sung in his rich, baritone voice with his eyes fixed upon her face. She had seen him in the way the islanders treated him, with respect and affection; in the way he had talked to young children and handled a tiny bird; in the tenderness with which he had spoken of his family.

And in the way he had kissed her. With passion and desire, yet never brutally, never as if he would take more than she wanted to give. And oh, *how* she wanted to give . . .

The only thing she couldn't understand about him was why he objected so strongly to her search for Iphigenia.

The tears were falling fast now but she couldn't be bothered to wipe them away. She sat down on the beach, drawing her knees up to her chin. What was she to do? Give up her search and go home, as Lukas had so brutally suggested? Take herself away, out of his sight for ever, and make sure they never met again? The idea was a bleak one, bleak and painful. Did that mean she had fallen in love?

No! she thought, thumping the sand with her fist. No, I won't fall in love with him! I won't.

"Hi, there. How's the happy bride?"

The voice made her jump. She turned quickly and saw Gil smiling down at her. Alix stared at him and drew in a deep, shuddering breath.

"I'm not," she said, her voice shaking.

"Not what?" he enquired cheerfully. "Not a bride, or not happy?" He looked at her more closely and his smile faded. "No, you're not, are you? What's the matter?" Gracefully, he folded his body down beside her and slipped his arm around her shoulders. "Tell Uncle Gil all about it."

"Oh . . ."

She hadn't meant to. The story of her grandfather and Iphigenia had been too precious to blurt out to strangers. She would have told Lukas, but for his hostility and but for her grandfather's warning about the possibility of trouble for Iphigenia. But when Gil looked at her with his blue eyes full of sympathy and interest, when he spoke in that warm, coaxing voice, she could keep it suppressed no longer. She told him all of it — about Ian McConnell, away in New Zealand, too crippled to make the journey he longed to make; about her promise to come here and find out what had happened to his sweetheart all those years ago; about Lukas's offer of help, which had turned out to be no help at all.

"But why did he offer?" Gil asked, and she

shrugged her shoulders. She had not mentioned the visit to the monastery where Lukas's grandmother lived, nor the reason for their spurious 'engagement'. Better, perhaps, to let him think they had recognised each other from the Minos, or even that they'd known each other much better in London — perhaps quarrelled — and that she'd come here to find him, as well as Iphigenia.

"He just wanted to make sure I never found her," she said bleakly. "And he would have succeeded, too. He *has* succeeded. No one will help me now, once he's told them all our engagement is off." She stared out at the darkening sea, her eyes filling once again with tears.

"And how do you feel about that?" Gil asked after a moment.

"About the engagement? Oh, that was a mistake from the beginning," she said tonelessly. "I should never have agreed to it."

There was a short silence. Gil's arm was still around her shoulders. She thought of Lukas, slipping his arm round her at the party to keep her warm. It had been like being enfolded in soft fleece, as if his warmth had spread through her whole body.

Gil's arm was just an arm, no more than that.

"How would you like me to help you?" he asked softly.

Alix turned and looked into his face.

"You?"

"Why not? I speak Greek — not as well as our

restaurant-owning friend, but well enough. I've got a car, I've got the time. I'd enjoy it." He squeezed her shoulders slightly. "And I think you're rather in need of a friend just now."

The tears overflowed. Alix looked away and bit her lip, trying to keep them in check. Why should she start crying again, just because someone had offered to help her?

"I'd like that very much," she said shakily. "If you're sure you don't mind?"

"I told you — I'd like to." He smiled at her, his eyes crinkling at the corners. "I was fascinated by your engagement, it seemed so romantic. But *this* story, why, it's even more romantic. The old soldier, yearning all these years through a loveless marriage for the beautiful Cretan girl he left behind —"

"It wasn't a loveless marriage," Alix interrupted. "He and Grandma had a good life. It's only since she died —"

"— and then sending his favourite grandchild to search on his behalf," Gil continued, evidently carried away. He stopped and grinned. "Sorry. It's my romantic soul. I'm incurably sentimental, I'm afraid."

"It's all right." It wasn't often, Alix thought, that you would find a man who could admit to such a trait. Certainly Lukas wouldn't! But even as she thought that, she saw again a picture of him standing with a small bird cradled gently in his hands and saying *"Ochi, ochi . . .* Too small, too small . . ." to a clamour of children.

208

"So it's agreed, then," Gil went on, and she looked at him, momentarily startled. For a few seconds she had been back on that terrace, watching Lukas, feeling — what? Abruptly, she thrust the picture from her mind and smiled at her companion.

"It's agreed," he repeated. "Tomorrow we start the search again — but this time we'll find her."

"Agreed," Alix said, and put out her hand.

Gil took it and held it between both of his for a moment. Then he got up, drawing her to her feet. For a moment they stood together, and then he planted a brief kiss on her brow and said lightly, "Let's go and eat. I'm starving, and I'm willing to bet you haven't eaten properly all day."

"Oh, but —" Alix had been about to say that she'd had plenty to eat, that she wasn't hungry at all. But even as she began to speak, she realised that she too was ravenously hungry and that it was, after all, several hours since the rabbit and chips.

"It's all right," he said. "We won't go to Lukas's taverna. There's another one round the headland, right on the seashore and every bit as good. We'll go there."

Keeping hold of her hand, he led her along the shore. The village was quiet, most of the visitors already eating in the different restaurants, with just a few wandering along the promenade. With any luck, Alix thought, Lukas's taverna will be busy and we shall be able to cross the bridge without being seen.

· It was almost dark. The toads were croaking and the taverna was lit with candles on each table, the waiters and waitresses hurrying back and forth with their trays. The tables under the vines on the terrace were all, it seemed, occupied by couples who were deeply in love as if they had been placed there for effect. Beyond, in the brightly lit kitchen, Alix could see the cooks working over their chopping boards and steaming pans. Lukas's uncle was there, short and tubby, and his plump wife Lita. There was no sign at all of Lukas.

She drew a deep breath of relief. They were almost past the door. In another moment, they would be out of sight. And then a shadow detached itself from the wall and Lukas's voice vibrated through the air.

"Not patronising us tonight?"

Alix stopped dead. She could feel Gil's fingers tighten around hers, urging her on, but she was powerless to move. Lukas moved into the light that spilled from the lanterns hung among the vines. She saw his face, dark and cold as an Arctic night.

"Did you expect us to?" she asked, using the term 'us' only because she was with Gil at that moment.

Lukas let his eyes move icily over her face, then turned and gave Gil the same chilling assessment. Although her heart was quaking,

Alix stood her ground, but when his gaze turned to her again she felt a stab of anguish deep in her heart. Oh Lukas, Lukas, she thought, we could have been so much to each other . . .

"I expect nothing of you any more," he said quietly. "Are you going to take my advice and leave Crete?"

Alix faced him. "Not until we've found Iphigenia."

"I see. You don't care that your interference might ruin her life, that nothing will ever be the same for her again?"

"I don't believe it," she said. "You've told me nothing that convinces me that's true."

He stared at her again and this time there was contempt in his eyes.

"Do I have to tell you?" he asked scathingly. "Why don't you just go back to some of the other people in whose lives you've interfered, and ask them?"

He did not wait for an answer. As if the scene were too much for him, he turned on his heel and disappeared again into the darkness. And Alix was left staring at the spot where he had been.

The toads croaked loudly. A few people walked past, laughing. And Gil tugged gently at her hand.

"Come," he said. "Let's go and eat. Forget him, Alix. He was bad news. But you still have plenty of time left to find Iphigenia."

She nodded and let him lead her away into the

twilight. But although she laughed and talked during the meal, although Gil took pains to make the evening a success, she could not rid herself of the anguish that had stabbed her heart when she looked into Lukas's eyes and recognised the love they could have shared.

Love now lost for ever.

At Gil's suggestion, they went back to Sellia next morning to begin the search all over again. Once again aware of the possible need for caution, Alix impressed upon him that the real purpose of their enquiries must remain secret. They were looking for Iphigenia on behalf of a friend in England, nothing more. No mention of the war, soldiers or New Zealand was to be made.

"It doesn't make it easy," Gil complained, but he acquiesced and they went into the taverna where she had first begun.

The same old men were sitting there, almost as if they had never moved, but Alix had an uncomfortable feeling that some of them had moved as far as the taverna in Plakias for her engagement party. Their faces were cautious, their eyes suspicious as they listened to Gil and looked at the sketch. One by one, they shook their heads, but Alix was aware of a difference between these and the old men she and Lukas had met in the other village. Those men had looked carefully at the picture, had produced spectacles in order to see it more closely, had discussed and argued with each other over who it might be.

These simply shook their heads and said *"Ochi."* No. This was nobody they knew, or had ever known. They did not need to discuss it to be sure.

Or perhaps they had already been told not to discuss it.

"He's been here already," she said angrily as she and Gil stepped out again into the bright sunshine. "He's told them not to say anything. We don't have a chance of finding her now."

"Mm. I certainly got the impression they knew and just weren't telling." He looked thoughtfully at the sketch. "I must say, she was quite a beauty. Not a face you'd forget in a hurry."

"Except that it was fifty years ago. She can't have looked like that for years." Alix took back the sketch, gazed at it and sighed. "If only I knew what was behind it all. Why he's so anxious that I shouldn't find her. Why he thinks it would ruin her life." She turned to Gil, her green eyes filled with distress. "It must mean she's in some kind of trouble. What else can it be? And that's just what my grandfather wants to know. He wants to help her, if she needs it."

"And so he shall," Gil said with determination. "Look, Alix, there are ways of finding things out, ways that super-annuated canteen cook can't interfere with. But it means a visit to Heraklion and a couple of phone calls to people I know in England. Why don't you leave it to me?"

He looked at her, his eyes bright. "I'll do it this afternoon — drive over and get things moving. You take the afternoon off — you look exhausted."

Alix had to admit that she was. She had spent a restless night and had fallen heavily asleep at six, only to be woken an hour later by the shrill tone of her alarm clock. The search for Iphigenia had tangled itself through her dreams, incoherently muddled with distorted snatches of memory of her day with Lukas. The tiny bird, the kiss by the waterfall, the old men under the olive tree — all had played their part, leaving her mind almost feverish rather than rested.

"I don't know," she said doubtfully. "I feel it's something I ought to do myself. I promised Grandfather —"

"You promised you'd find her. There were no conditions laid down about how you should do that, not from what you've told me. Only that you needed to be careful not to offend the family." Gil's voice was persuasive. "Asking my help doesn't go against anything your grandfather would have wanted — indeed, I'm sure he'd far rather you asked my help than that of a local man who's already admitted he's highly prejudiced against you. And just why should he *be* prejudiced?" He looked very serious. "Don't you think you may already, quite unwittingly of course, trodden on some rather sensitive toes? Don't you think that his reaction proves that Iphigenia may already be in trouble? I'd say it's imperative we find her, and quickly. She may need help."

Alix stared at him. "Oh, Gil — do you really think so?"

"I think it's entirely possible, yes. I don't like the way those men in the taverna were behaving. They looked extremely furtive to me. Something's going on, Alix, make no mistake about that, and it's up to us to put a stop to it." He waited for a moment. "And when we've found Iphigenia — as I'm determined we will — there's a small proposition I want to put to you."

"To me?" Alix felt dazed. "A proposition?" A tiny alarm bell rang in her mind. "What sort of proposition? If you're attaching strings to your help —"

He laughed, his eyes crinkling in that attractive way that made her feel ashamed of even a momentary doubt. "No strings, Alix — and certainly not of the kind you may be thinking of, though I won't deny that I find you a very attractive young woman and I'd like to talk about that sometime. But I respect and admire you too much to try to take advantage of this situation. No, the proposition I'd like to make is one that would help both Iphigenia and your grandfather. Bring their story to its proper conclusion. It shouldn't be allowed to just tail away, don't you think?"

Once again, Alix felt a twinge of doubt. The matter seemed to have been taken out of her hands. Things were happening too quickly. She looked into the clear blue eyes.

"I don't know. I think Grandfather just wants to know she's all right. He doesn't want —"

"And that's just what we're going to be able to tell him," Gil said bracingly. "And after that — well, we'll see. People can always change their minds, you know. But it'll be entirely for the two of them to decide. And the main thing is to find her. So I'll dash off to Heraklion and make those phone calls, OK?"

"You could call from Plakias —" she began, but he shook his head.

"There's someone in Heraklion I need to see as well. And that's where all the records will be kept. Just leave it all to me, Alix. I know what I'm doing." He smiled at her. "I've had plenty of experience, believe me."

Experience? Alix looked at him, puzzled. His eyes were crinkling again with what looked like laughter, a secret amusement. Yet he'd sounded so serious — as if he were genuinely concerned for Iphigenia.

"Are you sure you don't mind?" she asked doubtfully, and Gil shook his head. His eyes were gleaming.

"Mind? Alix, I'm just beginning to enjoy myself! I love something like this, a challenge I can really get my teeth into. And it certainly beats sitting on the beach reading the latest thriller." He put his arm round her shoulders and squeezed them tightly. "Don't you worry about me. I'll soon tell you if I'm bored. Now,

I'll just run you back to Plakias and then I'll be off."

"But there's no need to do that. I can walk back through the olive groves."

"Through the olive groves?" He glanced doubtfully down the hill. "Are you sure?"

"Yes. I know the way. And it'll be pleasantly cool under the trees."

"I really think you ought to go and rest," he began, but Alix shook her head.

"I shall as soon as I get back to my apartment, but I'd like a walk now. I spent too long sitting in a car yesterday." Too long sitting close to Lukas, she thought. "I need the exercise and fresh air."

And there was something else she needed too, but this was something she wasn't yet ready to mention to anyone.

"Well, all right." He still looked doubtful. "But let's get something to eat first. It's almost lunchtime."

At the end of the village was another taverna, this one obviously catering much more for tourists although as yet there were few in evidence. Gil led the way on to a large terrace, set with tables and chairs, and they sat down and ordered salads.

The food was good, but Alix found herself unable to concentrate on it. To please Gil, she nibbled at as much as she could, and then pushed the plate away. He was clearly as ready as she to start the afternoon, and they parted outside the little restaurant, agreeing to meet in the evening to discuss progress.

What was he going to do? she wondered. What ways did he know of finding people on Crete? What experience had he already had of such searches?

She realised suddenly that she had no idea what his job was. Did he have something to do with the Army? Intelligence, perhaps?

She felt a sudden twinge of fear. What had she started?

She stared after his car, stepping forward as if to wave to him to stop. But it disappeared round the corner and her hand fell back to her side. Don't be ridiculous! she scolded herself. You're letting your imagination run away with you. And now's your chance to do what you want to do.

Ever since last night, her conscience had been troubling her. She had been unable to stop thinking of Lukas's intention to tell his family the truth about their engagement. *His* version of the truth. She squirmed inside at the thought of their disappointment, of the anger they would feel, the hostility towards her.

It was poor reward for the welcome they had extended. But worst of all was the thought of the old grandmother.

Alix could hardly bear the thought of her distress — and distress she knew there would be, for it must follow on the heels of such delight as the old woman had shown. If only I could explain, she had thought miserably, if only I could tell her myself.

But you can, memory reminded her. Lukas's grandmother speaks English. Only a little, perhaps, and that rusty from long disuse, but perhaps she still retained enough to be able to understand the story of two lovers separated by war. Especially if Alix showed her the sketch of Iphigenia and the photograph of the young, laughing Ian McConnell.

She might even, as Alix had at first supposed, remember Iphigenia herself. They must, surely, have known one another.

But most important was to settle her mind, to remove the disappointment and distrust that must inevitably follow Lukas's disclosures. And to reassure her that her grandson was no opportunist, ready to snatch a kiss from any girl he met by chance, but a gentleman who would never take advantage.

Alix stopped with a small gasp. Was that really what she wanted to tell Lukas's grandmother? Did she really want to show him in a good light? Was she going on his behalf or her own?

Neither, she thought. This is for the old lady herself. Yes, and maybe for my own sake, to ease my own conscience. And to do that I've got to tell the truth.

She remembered their kisses, in the doorway, at the engagement party, by the waterfall. Three kisses which were all she had of him, kisses that had been like storms through her heart, kisses that had melted her body and driven fire through her veins, sending shafts of desire through every quivering muscle. Kisses that had been mutual. Shared.

Lukas had never forced himself upon her, never touched her unless she too had desired it. Her desire must have shown in her eyes, as his had done. Her aura must have been as powerful as his.

Her heart ached again at the thought of what they could have been to each other; of what they had lost.

For a few moments she stood quite still at the top of the little path leading down to the old monastery. Then she stiffened her back, squared her shoulders and began to walk down through the olive groves.

The old monastery stood dreaming quietly in the sunlit groves. Alix stood with her hand on the crumbling walls, gazing down at the curving bay. What a place this must have been for the monks who had lived and prayed here. What stories these old stones could tell! She sensed the serene tranquillity that pervaded the ancient building, and felt a deep rapport with the old woman who lived in this beautiful place.

Perhaps this was why she chose to live here, away from the village. Perhaps she loved the peace too much to move back into the life of the community.

A sound made her turn quickly and she saw Lukas's grandmother come out from a cluster of olive trees. She carried a basket over her arm and was scattering corn for the hens who scratched and clucked about her feet. She saw Alix and her old face cracked into a beaming smile. Setting the basket down, she hurried forward, her hands held out in welcome.

He hasn't told her yet, Alix thought. She thinks we're still engaged.

Her heart sank at the thought of breaking the news to the old woman and she understood why Lukas had been so reluctant to disappoint her. The thought of removing the pleasure from that delighted face was not one she relished. But it would have to be done, and she mentally cursed Lukas for making it necessary.

"Please," she said, breaking in on the torrent of words falling from the old woman's lips. "Please, I don't understand! *Dhen Katalaveno.*" She gazed helplessly into the old eyes. "I thought you could speak English!"

The grandmother laughed and shook her head. "I forget. You speak not Greek. My English bad, very bad — but I try." She clasped Alix's hands in her own and shook them up and down. "Is good you come here," she said, obviously having to think to choose the words. "Good you come to me."

You won't think that when I tell you why I came, Alix thought sadly. But she braced herself and said, "I wanted to talk to you. There are things I have to say."

"Things to say." The old head nodded. "*Neh.* We talk much. Two women, we both love

Lukas." She laughed again and shook her head as if chiding a mischievous child. "Lukas is a bad boy! He tells nobody he has sweetheart. Ach!"

This was proving worse than Alix had anticipated. Lukas's grandmother was evidently looking forward to a tête-à-tête with the new member of the family. She would be wanting to know all about their supposed 'courtship' in London, their plans for the wedding, probably even how many children they planned to have . . . At the thought of children, Alix's face flamed and she felt a deep pain twisting inside. To have Lukas's children . . .

The old woman was tugging at her hands, urging Alix to accompany her. She wants to feed me again, Alix thought, beginning to feel slightly hysterical. In another minute she'll be getting out the family album and showing me pictures of Lukas as a baby, naked on a rug.

The grandmother drew her towards the door of the rooms she used as a cottage. The chairs and small table were still there; presumably she ate her own meals outside. She indicated that Alix should sit down and pushed quite firmly on her shoulders.

"But I —" Alix tried to summon up the words to tell her the truth. I can't let this go any further, she thought desperately. She's got to know. But the chattering voice had relapsed into Greek again and before she could break in, the grandmother had turned and bustled through the door to disappear in the dimness beyond.

Alix felt totally helpless. She sat still, gazing at the view of the bay, wondering what to do next. The thought of breaking in on that happy volubility and destroying the old woman's pleasure was acutely painful, yet she knew it must be done. And done before she was forced to accept any further hospitality.

I'd like to kill you for this, Lukas Stavroulakis, she thought, and made up her mind. She got up and followed the grandmother in through the doorway.

The old woman had gone through a further door, into a small kitchen. She was filling a tin kettle with water and setting it on a small portable gas stove. She looked round at Alix and smiled and then, moving with unexpected swiftness, slipped past her and outside again.

She had gone for more water. Alix made to follow her, then stopped. This wasn't something that could be discussed over a well or spring, or wherever she had gone. Perhaps after all it would be better if she allowed the grandmother to make some coffee. She would need a hot drink to allay the shock that Alix feared her news was going to be. Perhaps I shouldn't tell her at all, she thought, grabbing at straws. I wouldn't like to be responsible for her having some kind of attack . . .

No. That was the coward's way out. She could not sit here and drink the old woman's coffee and eat her food and then simply walk away. She could not leave without having told her the truth.

Alix wandered unhappily back into the main room. She glanced about it, thinking of that first time when she had come in here — was it really so short a time ago? — and been discovered by Lukas. It had all stemmed from there. If he had not found her that afternoon, none of this would have happened. None of the lies would have been told and the anguish of the past few days would have been avoided.

Well, this time at least she was here by invitation, even though the invitation was itself a part of that lie. She looked at the few ornaments in the room and, driven by the curiosity which encourages any visitor to look at family photographs, picked up the framed portrait of the young girl in a wedding dress.

It was Iphigenia.

Iphigenia . . .

Alix almost dropped it. The blood roared in her ears as she stared at the beautiful young face. A few years older than in her grandfather's sketch, but unmistakably the same girl. She gazed out from the photograph, her dark hair elaborately dressed, the lace falling like a cloud of tiny snowflakes about her face, and in her eyes there was a strange, ethereal quality, a joy that was touched with sadness, as if haunted by a memory that could never be erased.

Iphigenia . . .

Dazed, she let her eyes move over the rest of

the pictures. A matching portrait of a man, tall and dark, dressed in the dramatic Cretan style, with tall boots, full black trousers and waistcoat. Her bridegroom, no doubt, the man to whom she had been betrothed. Had he known about Ian McConnell?

The rest were of family groups. Children, arranged solemnly in order of height. Sons, daughters, grandchildren. Lukas himself. And, slightly apart from the others and set at an angle to face the wedding portrait as if to let the couple smile into each other's eyes, the photograph of a man . . .

Through the pounding in her ears, Alix heard a footfall. Still holding the two photographs, she turned and stared into the eyes of the old woman who stood in the doorway.

The same eyes. Iphigenia's eyes.

They gazed at each other for a long moment. Then Iphigenia stepped forward and Alix saw that her face was creased into a thousand tiny wrinkles. She took the photograph of herself and looked at it, nodding slowly and smiling.

"You," she said, pointing at the picture, and Alix frowned slightly before realising that the old woman had her pronouns mixed.

"You," she said, smiling at the unconscious ridiculousness which did nothing to destroy the tenderness of the moment. She pointed first at the photograph, then at her companion. "You. Iphigenia."

The old woman looked surprised that Alix

knew her name, then she nodded vigorously. She turned and lifted the matching portrait. "My husband. Georgios."

"He looks a fine man," Alix said politely. She was acutely conscious of the third picture, the one she held in her hand. She lifted it so that they could both see and then, deciding that there was no other way, said quite simply, "Ian. My grandfather."

Another crease added itself to Iphigenia's seamed face as she frowned a little, trying to understand the words Alix had used. But there was no doubt that she had recognised his name. She stared at the old photograph, much folded and creased before it had been framed, and then at Alix. Carefully, she laid down the pictures of herself and her husband and took the photograph of Ian McConnell. Her fingers held it caressingly and she stroked the smiling face, and then looked again at Alix. Her old eyes misted.

"Ian? Your . . . grandfather?"

"Yes." Alix gazed at her, trying to find the words that would convey her message to Iphigenia's limited understanding of English. "The father of my mother. He sent me here to find you. He wants to know that you are well." She paused. "He has never forgotten you."

There was no doubt now that Iphigenia understood. The old face, which seemed to have as many seams and creases as it was possible for a face to have, crumpled into an even greater mass of minute wrinkles. The old eyes, still dark, still expressive, shone with tears. She gazed at Alix, who felt the tears come hot to her own eyes, and then she looked again at the picture, at the smiling young New Zealander she had loved half a century ago.

Suddenly, with a swift, impulsive movement, she brought the photograph to her lips and kissed it. Then she held it against her breast.

"Ian," she said simply. "We loved."

Alix tried to swallow the lump that had risen to her throat. "I know."

Iphigenia reached out and touched the wedding portrait of her husband. "My man. We loved." She shrugged and looked again at the picture of the laughing young soldier. She touched the pictures of her family. Of the children, ranged in age. The grandchildren. Lukas. "We have children. Many children. We love. But —" she looked again at Ian's face "— but not as Ian and Iphigenia."

Alix nodded. The moment was overwhelmingly poignant. She thought of the long years that these two had spent apart, the two marriages that had taken place on opposite sides of the world. Marriages that had endured, had been happy, marriages blessed with families. Yet what could marriage between the two of them have been, had it been allowed to happen?

Nobody had prevented their marriage. Fate, two different cultures, an honour strictly observed on both sides — these had kept the two apart. And at the same time, had kept their love true, a love that had remained pure, a love that had damaged no one.

She looked again at Iphigenia's photograph, at the eyes that were haunted by a memory that could never be erased.

The memory of that love never had been erased.

The old woman murmured something and slipped out of the cottage again. Alix started after her, then halted. She needs to be alone, she thought. She needs time to think, to come to terms with my appearance. She needs to think about her husband and about Grandfather.

She turned again to the photographs, unwilling somehow to let them go, and when she heard another step at the door she turned, smiling, expecting to see Iphigenia once more at the door.

But instead the light was shadowed by the dark, bulky figure of a man. He stood blocking her way, his face obscured. But Alix needed no clue to tell who it was. And when he spoke, it was with the deep, baritone voice she had known she would hear.

"This is where we came in, I think."

His tone was ominous. She felt a tremor of fear as he moved inside, shifting his body so that the light fell once again across his dark features. She looked up at him and saw the hard anger in his eyes, an anger that did not diminish when he saw what she held in her hands.

"So now you know," he said. "You've found

Iphigenia." He took the photograph from her fingers and examined it, his dark face shadowed, unreadable. "Iphigenia. My grandmother."

Chapter Eleven

Alix turned. She picked up the second photograph, the one that had been standing beside that of Iphigenia. The photograph of a young New Zealand soldier, blue-eyed and laughing.

"And do you know who this one is?" she asked quietly. "It's my grandfather. The soldier who loved her and had to leave her. *Had* to leave her. The man who loved her for the rest of his life and only wants to know that she's happy and well cared for in her old age." She looked up at Lukas, her green eyes brilliant with tears and the smouldering fire of her own anger. "How *can* you say that she shouldn't be told he still thinks of her? Who are you to make her decisions for her?"

Lukas stared at her. "Your *grandfather?*"

"Yes. Of course. Why else do you think I'd be so anxious to find her?"

His brows came together in a heavy frown. "You mean you'd do this to your own grandfather?"

Alix's patience snapped. "Do *what,* for heaven's sake? Lukas, ever since we started this you've been dropping these heavy hints about the dreadfulness of what I'm doing. What *is* so terrible about it? Why do you hate the idea so much? All I'm doing is trying to bring some peace of mind to two old people who clearly still think about each other." She gestured at the photographs. "It's obvious that your grand-mother still loves him. Just as he still loves her. They may both have been married since, they may have been happy in those marriages, but they've never lost their feeling for each other. What's so wrong with that? It's a lovely story."

"A lovely story," he repeated slowly, but his voice vibrated with suppressed fury. "Yes. That's what it is, isn't it. That's *all* it is to you. *A lovely story.* And you'll take it and make use of it and broadcast it everywhere for other people to enjoy, people who've got nothing better to do than pry into the lives of others, who —"

"*What in God's name are you talking about?*" Alix stamped her foot and grabbed him by the arms, shaking him in her exasperation. "*What people?* What mixed-up, twisted, utterly *stupid* idea have you got in that warped mind of yours? I've told you, all I want to do —"

"Quiet!" he said sharply, and she stopped and stared at him, shocked by his tone. Then she heard footsteps across the yard and realised that Iphigenia was coming back with the water. She bit her lip, feeling the tears in her eyes. *Now* what was she to do?

Apparently Lukas had already made the deci-sion. His fingers around her wrist, he drew her towards the door. They came out into the dappled sunlight and met Iphigenia coming out of the shade of the big olive tree.

"Don't say anything now," he muttered in Alix's ear. "We've got to sort this out. I'll tell her we can't stay — there's been a phone call for you in the taverna and you've got to go back."

Alix tried to tug her wrist from his grasp, but his fingers tightened. "Just don't try it, Alix," he grated. "If you try to tell her now, I'll override anything you say and you'll be all the sorrier afterwards, understand?"

"So you're descending to threats, are you?" she sneered. "As well as more lies."

"There's no lie — there *has* been a call for you. As to threats — yes, if you like. I tell you, I *will not* have my grandmother upset by this." He lifted his head and smiled at the old woman who was coming across the clearing towards them, her face slightly puzzled as if she could see that there was something not right. "Grandmother," he said in English, "I'm so sorry we can't stay and have coffee with you. Alix is needed in the village — a phone call from her boss." He spoke quickly in Greek, presumably repeating the words and Iphigenia's face cleared and she nodded and smiled at Alix. She answered her grandson in their own language and then put out her hands to take Alix's. Lukas released her wrist and Alix, feeling like a criminal, let the old woman touch her fingers.

"Come later," Iphigenia said, her black eyes tender. "Come soon. We talk again."

"Yes," Alix said, meaning every word. "I'll come. We'll talk again. Soon." Lukas repossessed her hand and drew her to the edge of the clearing and she turned and repeated her words. "I'll come."

Iphigenia nodded and waved. She stood watching as they walked away down the path and then they turned a corner and she was out of sight. But not yet out of earshot, and Alix waited until they had descended for a considerable distance before she stopped and planted her feet firmly on the ground.

Lukas turned and faced her.

"Right," she said, her voice as firm as she could make it, though it still quivered a little with suppressed anger and frustration. "Now perhaps you'll tell me what all this is about. I thought you were going to tell your grandmother the truth?"

"I was." His eyes betrayed his own anger. "That's why I came up here this afternoon. Instead, I found you, poking and prying about just as you did before. Only this time, unfortunately, you found what you were looking for."

"I was not poking and prying," Alix said coldly. "I was there by invitation. I came to tell her the truth myself, to make peace with her and my conscience. She took me indoors to have coffee and then went for more water. *She* didn't mind me looking at the photographs."

"Why should she?" he said nastily. "She had no idea who you really are."

233

"She does now." Alix faced him squarely. "I've told her about my grandfather. She knows he never forgot her. And I'm glad. It's made her very happy."

"*Glad?*" He spat out the word as if it were something disgusting. "*Happy?* Alix, how can you believe that? How can you take these people's lives and blazon them abroad —"

"What are you talking about? What do you mean? Lukas, you keep saying these things and I just don't understand. All I wanted to do was let Iphigenia know that my grandfather is still alive and thinks of her. He asked me to come here, to find her and make sure she wasn't in need. He wanted her to know he'd never forgotten her, and if there was anything she wanted —" She felt the tears forcing themselves into her throat, spilling from her eyes, and stopped, holding out her hands with a helpless gesture. "Obviously I had to go carefully, she might still be married, there might have been trouble caused in the past — he knew she was betrothed, although her fiancé was missing. But he just wanted to *know*. What's so terrible about that?"

"There's nothing terrible about it," Lukas said quietly. "If that were all you meant to do, I'd think it a wonderful thing for her. She *has* never forgotten him — you can see that from the photograph. No, it's not that. It's the other plan you had for her. You — and your slimy boss."

"My *boss?*" Once again, Alix felt bewilderment rock through her. "You said that before. And you just told me that my boss had phoned me here. But that's impossible. He doesn't know where to contact me — why should he? He has nothing to do with it."

If looks could truly wither, Alix would have shrivelled and died on the spot. Lukas's dark eyes raked her with such bitter scorn that she could almost feel them on her skin, grazing it as if with the touch of coarse sandpaper. She flinched under their impact but did not move, nor did she turn her own eyes away.

"It's impossible," she said firmly. "My boss has no interest in this whatsoever."

"None at all?" His voice was bitingly sarcastic. "You've never even discussed it with him?"

"Of course not." Her bewilderment grew. "Lukas, what —"

"Not even when you were on the beach together last night?" he continued, raising his voice above hers. "When you sat with his arms around you, when he kissed you, when you walked past my aunt's taverna holding hands? Or perhaps you had other things on your minds just then, and later, when he saw you back to your apartment. Perhaps you —"

"Lukas, *stop* it!" Once again, she reached out and grabbed his arms, shaking him in an attempt to halt the flow of bitter words. "What on earth gave you the idea that Gil is my boss? He isn't! I never even met him until I came here."

Lukas stopped abruptly. He stared at her. His brows came together again and his jaw dropped slightly. If the situation hadn't been so desperate, Alix thought wryly, it would have been comical.

"You deny that he's your boss?"

"Yes. Of course he isn't. My boss is a man called John Kitchener and he's in London, editing a magazine."

"So you do admit you're a journalist."

"Yes. Why shouldn't I?" What all this had to do with Iphigenia, Alix had no idea, but it seemed to be important to Lukas, so she went on. "I've worked on *Science Today* for the past three years. I'm a scientific journalist. I have a degree in physics. Didn't you know all this? I used to bring scientists into your restaurant for lunch."

"I thought they were authors," he muttered.

"Well, so they were. Writers, anyway. Scientists can write, you know," she added sardonically.

There was a short silence. Alix watched Lukas as he assimilated this knowledge. Then he looked at her again and she saw to her dismay that the inimical expression was still there.

"So perhaps you can explain why our fair-headed friend is as keen as you are to find my grandmother. For someone you only met a couple of days ago, you certainly looked very friendly on the beach last night. I presume you told him all about your search."

"Yes, I did as a matter of fact. Why not? I needed someone who could speak Greek and you weren't going to help me any more. Not that you ever did," she added pointedly. "And as for my degree of 'friendliness' with Gil — which was nothing more than a comforting arm around my shoulder when I was feeling a bit depressed — you're a fine one to talk, when you announced our engagement within minutes of meeting me!"

Lukas's lips twitched slightly and she saw that the barb had gone home. *"Touché,"* he murmured, and her heart lifted a little, but the hardness was back in his voice as he said, "Nevertheless, you're willing to accept his help, even though you know perfectly well what he'll do with it. Or is that the bargain you've struck with him?"

"Bargain?" she echoed, nonplussed. "I don't understand."

"Oh, come on, Alix!" he snapped, clearly losing patience. "Of course you understand! A man like Gil Tarrant isn't going to let a story like this pass him by. He's going to make the most of it. He'll milk it for every drop he can squeeze out. All right, I'll accept that you weren't working for him before you came here — perhaps not even until last night. But you most definitely are now. And I might as well tell you here and now, that if you do, if you sink to his level and lift so much as one tiny fingernail to harass my grandmother over this business, I shall make it my personal business to hound you both off this island — yes, and I'll enjoy every minute of it. Every *minute*." He stared at her and she saw the tormented darkness in his eyes. "I wish you'd never come here, Alix Berringer," he said in a low voice. "I wish you'd never come to this island with your sketches and your photographs and your tear-jerking tale. But I tell you this — if you had to come, and if I had to meet you, I'd rather it happened this way than any other. At least I can save my grandmother from being made an exhibition of!"

There was a long silence. Then Alix said carefully, choosing each word, "Will you please tell me what you are talking about? Just who is Gil Tarrant? Why does he make you so angry?"

"Oh, for heaven's *sake!*" Lukas exclaimed. "You're not going to tell me you don't know who Gil Tarrant is!"

"But I don't."

"You've never heard of him?" His voice was unbelieving. "You've never heard of *Meeting Point?*"

"*Meeting Point?*" She shook her head. "What is it? Some sort of dating agency?"

Lukas gave her a long look. His dark eyes searched hers. Steadily, she returned his gaze, determined not to let hers waver. At last, she thought, we're getting to the crux of this matter.

"*Meeting Point,*" Lukas said slowly, as if addressing a small child, "is a television programme. It came here from America, where apparently it's one of the biggest things since the moonshot. It brings people together — mothers and the children they gave up for adoption, fathers who've lost touch with their children, old friends who lost contact, perhaps through a quarrel or some tragic event, and have a story to tell. And old sweethearts who were parted years ago." He paused. "It doesn't bother about what happens to them afterwards, how they pick up the pieces of their lives again after all the razzamatazz. How the mothers and children come to terms with what's happened, how the fathers try to get involved with children to whom they're strangers, how the old sweethearts struggle with emotions they should have buried long before."

Alix drew a deep breath.

"And Gil Tarrant?"

"Gil Tarrant is the host of this programme. The well-loved, sincere host who brings these people together and looks on as they fall into each other's arms, wiping a surreptitious tear — which he makes sure the camera sees — from his eye as he does so." Lukas looked at her. "You can't have missed hearing about him, even if you've never seen the programme. He's the hottest thing on television for years. He's been in all the papers, on all the chat shows, talking about this damned programme, talking about himself."

Alix shook her head. "How long has this programme been running?"

"I don't know exactly — two months, three? What does —"

"I," Alix said quietly, "have been in New Zealand for three months."

There was another long silence. Lukas gave a little sigh. Then he said, "Can you explain, then, why he rang the taverna this afternoon to say that he wants to contact you urgently? Why my uncle, who runs a hotel in Plakias, has received a booking for a television crew? Why your friend Gil Tarrant was in a travel agency in Plakias not an hour ago, trying to organise a flight from New Zealand?"

"He was doing *what?*"

"You heard," Lukas said heavily.

"But I didn't —" Alix began wildly. "I never — he offered to help me, that's all. He said he was going to Heraklion, he knew ways of tracing people, he had contacts —"

"Too right, he has," Lukas said grimly. "And he's pulling out all the stops. From what I can guess, he plans to get your grandfather over here to do the searching himself. He'll be taken around the villages in a big car, have his face in the island's newspapers and on TV. The whole story will be blazoned all over Crete and eventually someone will tell them who and where Iphigenia is. And her life will be exposed for everyone to see."

Alix stared at him. She had no doubt that he was speaking the truth. This was the challenge that Gil Tarrant had spoken of, that had made his eyes gleam. This was the proposition he planned to make.

Except that it was no proposition at all, because a man like Gil Tarrant, once in possession of a good story, would leave no stone unturned to make his plans come to fruition.

No wonder he had been so ready to help.

"Oh, Lukas," she whispered with dawning horror, "I never meant this to happen. Please, please believe me — I had no idea. I wouldn't for worlds —"

He looked at her. Once again, his eyes searched hers. The bronze rim glittered around his pupils and she met his gaze directly, honestly, willing him to believe her.

"You knew nothing?" he asked at last. "He said nothing to you about all this?"

"Nothing. Nothing at all. I swear it. Lukas, I would never, *never* —" Her voice trembled, shook, and then splintered into fragments as the tears came. "Oh, Lukas, I would never have asked his help if I'd known who he was. I hate that kind of thing as much as you do. People's lives being held up for entertainment, stories of pain and anguish used like a soap. I simply wanted to do as my grandfather asked — find Iphigenia and make sure she was happy. I didn't even intend to tell her about him, if it had been likely to cause difficulties. He just wanted to know. And help her if she needed it."

"Well, she doesn't need help," Lukas said with a return to his old grimness. "She has a family who look after her. She lives in the monastery because she's happy there and has a purpose, but the minute she becomes unable to look after herself there are a dozen homes ready to take her in."

"I know," Alix whispered. "But — but I still think she would like to know that he never forgot her. And he would like to know why she never wrote. That was their agreement — that she would contact him. He knew that if her fiancé had returned it could cause trouble for her, if he came back."

Lukas shrugged. "That's what happened — he came back. It was difficult, of course, for by then she had had the baby, but he accepted what had happened and took the child for his own. And they had a good and happy —"

Alix broke in, hardly able to believe her ears. "*Baby?* Child? What do you mean? What child?"

"Why," he said, "your grandfather's child, of course." And then, as she continued to stare at him. "My father."

"Your . . . *father?*" she breathed. "Your father is my grandfather's son?" She shook her head, trying to understand it. "So you and I are — cousins?"

"Of a sort," he said. It had obviously struck him before — probably the moment he had realised that the smiling New Zealander in his grandmother's photograph was Alix's grandfather. "Not full cousins, since we only share one grandparent. But yes, we are slightly related. Quarter cousins, I'd say."

"So Iphigenia was pregnant when he left the island," she said. "And he never knew. All these years and he never had the slightest idea." Her eyes filled with tears again and she looked up at

Lukas, shaking her head as the sadness over-whelmed her. "Oh, Lukas, such a waste!"

As if unable to help himself, he reached out and drew her against him. She leaned against his broad chest, enfolded in the warmth of his embrace, and the tears flowed. Then he said quietly, "It's sad that your grandfather never knew he had a son. But there was no waste, Alix. My grandfather — the man I've always considered my grandfather — loved Iphigenia too, he loved her enough to accept the child as his own and to give him all that he gave the rest of their children. They had a good life together. He made no objection when my grandmother sent my father to Edinburgh to study — she wanted him to know that he was partly Scots, for she knew that Ian McConnell had always been proud of his heritage and she couldn't bring herself to send him as far as New Zealand itself. And he was as happy as she when my father met and married my mother. I grieved when he died just as much as if he had been my true grandfather."

"And your father always knew the truth?"

"The whole family knew the truth," he said. "There was no shame. The New Zealanders were loved and respected here. They fought bravely to protect us. It wasn't their fault it went wrong. And for an island girl to fall in love with one . . . Nobody blamed her, Alix."

"It's a beautiful story," she said quietly. "But not one to be used as TV entertainment."

"No. And it's not just the family here on

Crete," he said. "It's my parents in England. The rest of my family there. They would all have been dragged into it too. Just think of it — that slimy, grinning TV host, trying to persuade them to appear on TV, nagging them to be in on his so-called surprise party, all dressed up in their best clothes, coming on stage to say their little piece about the two old people. Everyone weeping, and the studio audience baying for more while the couch potatoes sit at home with their Kleenex. And it would have happened. People like Tarrant use every trick in the book to make it impossible to refuse. I was determined to prevent that." He paused and looked down into her eyes. She saw that the warmth had returned, and felt, like a shock through her whole body, the force of his returning desire. His voice shook as he said, "And you really knew nothing of all this? You knew nothing of Gil Tarrant and *Meeting Point?*"

She shook her head. "Nothing."

"Oh, *Alix* . . ." His arms tightened about her. He bent his head and laid his lips on hers, and she felt a leaping joy as her love for him surged through her, the last barriers broken down, the final obstacles removed. "Alix, if you knew how I'd been feeling these past few days," he whispered, his mouth against her hair. "How I've found myself falling deeper and deeper in love with you, how I've fought it because I despised what I thought you were doing. Every time I thought I'd got you at arm's length, you did

244

something that made my heart turn over. So many things — the way you objected to all the lies, the way you held a child on your knee, the way you behaved in the little churches we visited, as if the atmosphere meant as much to you as it did to me. Even at the engagement party — it seemed so right. I found myself believing it was true, happy for it to be true. And most of all —" his arms tightened again and she felt his fingers in her hair and the tension in his body "— most of all was the way you made me feel whenever I came within a yard of your body. As if you were a magnet, drawing me towards you. As if at last I had found my woman, the one person I wanted to spend my life with.

"And every time I thought that," he continued, his lips moving gently over her face and eyes and ears, "something would remind me of your quest, and I would feel as if someone had plunged a knife deep into my heart and was slowly turning it . . . Oh, Alix, if only I hadn't believed you were working with Gil Tarrant. But could I be blamed for thinking what I did? You sat together on the plane — you were looking at a sketch of Iphigenia together, discussing it —"

"No!" she broke in. "That's not what happened. I was looking at it, yes, when Gil came and sat beside me, but it was sheer chance that he was given the seat beside mine. I dropped the sketch and he picked it up, that's all. He picked it up and looked at it." She stared at Lukas. "Do you mean to say you recognised your grandmother from that sketch of her as a young girl?"

He sighed. "I did. Because we have a similar sketch of her, you see. It hangs in my parents' house in London. I must have seen it every day throughout my childhood." His dark eyes searched hers. "Can you understand now why I was so shocked when I saw it in his hands? I knew who he was and I despised him and all he stood for. I knew you too. I hadn't realised — hadn't thought, I mean — that you worked for him, but when I saw you together on the plane, looking at my grandmother's picture — and then again, at the restaurant, talking about New Zealand — well, how could I help but put two and two together? I already knew you were a journalist, from the times you came into the Minos. I knew — or thought — you'd left *Science Today*. You hadn't been in for three months — the time during which *Meeting Point* had started — although Gil Tarrant had." He sighed and shook his head. "If only you'd been able to tell me your story before I saw you together in the taverna that first night! Seeing you here, apparently together, it was all too easy to make the wrong deduction."

"And now you know it was wrong. Horribly wrong," she said. "Oh, Lukas . . . All those things you've been doing — I've been doing them too. Falling in love with you, trying to deny it. Not wanting to get too close because of the effect you had on me. And it wasn't just a matter of a few feet any more — I don't have to be near

246

you at all now, to feel that all I want is to be in your arms like this, to feel your lips on mine and your body warm and close. I feel it all the time, no matter how near or far away you are." She pressed herself against him, moulding the contours of her body to his. "I love you, Lukas," she whispered. "I love you with all my heart."

She felt his response quiver through him, the big body trembling against her own. His desire was unmistakable. He kissed her with a deep, powerful passion, his mouth devouring her skin, her hair, her lips and tongue. His hands caught her against him, pressing against the small of her back, fingers splayed over her waist and buttocks, and he bent his head to her breasts.

"Alix," he muttered hoarsely. "Oh, my dear, darling, sweetest Alix . . ."

She whispered against his hair, murmuring words she scarcely knew she was saying, her emotions expressing themselves without reference to mind or brain, coming straight from her heart, straight from the love she knew was welling up inside her, a spring that would never be quenched. Her hands moved over his head, the thick curling hair tangling in her fingers, and she felt his lips once again on her throat, moving up her neck with a thousand tiny kisses, until they finally fastened once more, as if coming home, upon her mouth.

"Alix," he said at last, lifting his head and looking down into her eyes, "you will marry me, won't you? You will be my wife?"

"I will," she answered, and the words seemed to bring a solemnity to the moment, as if they were the marriage vow itself. "Oh, Lukas, I will!"

She saw the joy break out upon his face, the grimness and hostility gone for ever. And she knew that the same joy shone from her own eyes, a joy that expressed more than words as they gazed at each other.

He caught her hands in his, holding them close against his heart. "My darling, there's nothing I want more than to make love to you, here and now under the olive trees. But first, there are three things we have to do." He straightened out one of her fingers and held it up like a pointer. "One: we must give Tarrant his marching orders. Make it absolutely plain that he'd better forget the story of Iphigenia once and for all, and get him off Crete, hopefully for ever. Two: you must tell my grandmother all about your grandfather, and let her decide what to do next. My guess is that she'll weep a little, kiss his photograph when no one's looking and send him a message that she's never forgotten him — and leave it at that. They could never come together now, Alix. Too much has happened to them in the fifty years and more since they last met. They've grown too far apart."

Alix nodded. "I know. And I'm sure he wouldn't want any attempts made to get them to meet. He just wanted to know . . ." She looked up at him. "And the third?"

Lukas smiled down at her. He held her hands

248

closely and brought them to his lips to touch each fingertip with a lingering kiss that made her shiver. Then he said softly, "I want to make my lies come true, Alix. I want to woo you, as I told them I'd done at the engagement party. I want to give you flowers and chocolates and little gifts made of gold, and I want to court you as you should be courted. I want to wait to make love to you until our wedding night, and I want to make it as romantic and beautiful as I'll make the rest of our life together." His eyes were dark and bright, brown velvet overlaid with shimmering silk. "But, my darling Alix, I don't want to wait too long." He smiled. "Will three weeks be enough?"

"Enough?" she repeated, dazed by the emotion of his nearness, of the passion that quivered between them. "Enough for what?"

"To prepare for our wedding, of course!" he answered, and there was laughter in his voice. "Haven't you just said you'll marry me? And we'll need to prepare — a wedding in Crete is quite something. We'll have to get our families over too. There's a lot to do, Alix!"

"But —" She thought of her job in England. Would John Kitchener wait a little longer, while she had her unexpected honeymoon? She thought of her mother, who was about to discover a half-brother she had never known, a family she had no idea existed. She thought of Iphigenia, her old eyes filled with delight as she sat in the place of honour at the engagement party, her pleasure at welcoming Alix to the family.

She looked at Lukas and could find the words for none of these things. Instead, she laughed and shook her head, feeling the tears come yet again, and knew that this time they were tears of happiness and joy.

"Three weeks," she said, "is all the time in the world."

They stood together, enfolded in an embrace that told Alix she had come home at last. Home to the arms she had always longed for, the love that she had been seeking all her life. A love that accepted her for what she was — a woman, with all a woman's thoughts and emotions, with all a woman's desires and needs. A woman who, fulfilled by the right kind of love, could satisfy all the needs her man could ever have.

They exchanged a long, deep kiss that was as much a seal on their future as any marriage ceremony could ever be. And then Alix laid her head on Lukas's shoulder and gazed out through the whispering olive trees and across the shimmering blue bay.

Ian and Iphigenia had once stood like this, perhaps in this very spot. They had shared a love as deep as the one she was just beginning to share with Lukas. And that love had endured through over half a century, as the love between her and Lukas would endure.

And if those two lovers had never met, so she and Lukas could never have come together, for

Lukas would never have existed. That old, but not forgotten, love had blossomed and flowered. And its fruit would go on through the generations, through the children that she and Lukas would produce, through the tradition of the Cretan family blended with the Scots.

There'll be no end to it now, she thought, and in her heart she thanked and blessed her grandfather for sending her here. And the old woman up in the monastery for her patience and her faithfulness to a memory.

"Alix," Lukas said softly, and she lifted her face and offered her lips again for his kiss. And then, slowly, their arms wound about each other's waists, they began to walk on down through the sighing olive groves to the village of Plakias.

We hope you have enjoyed this Large Print book. Other G.K. Hall & Co. or Chivers Press Large Print books are available at your library or directly from the publishers.

For more information about current and upcoming titles, please call or write, without obligation, to:

G.K. Hall & Co.
P.O. Box 159
Thorndike, Maine 04986 USA
Tel. (800) 257-5157

OR

Chivers Press Limited
Windsor Bridge Road
Bath BA2 3AX
England
Tel. (0225) 335336

All our Large Print titles are designed for easy reading, and all our books are made to last.